OCEAN'S 11

OCEAN'S 11

A Novel by
Dewey Gram

Based on a Screenplay by
Ted Griffin

and a Screenplay by
Harry Brown and
Charles Lederer

AN ONYX BOOK

ONYX
Published by New American Library, a division of
Penguin Putnam Inc., 375 Hudson Street,
New York, New York 10014, U.S.A.
Penguin Books Ltd, 80 Strand,
London WC2R 0RL, England
Penguin Books Australia Ltd, Ringwood,
Victoria, Australia
Penguin Books Canada Ltd, 10 Alcorn Avenue,
Toronto, Ontario, Canada M4V 3B2
Penguin Books (N.Z.) Ltd, 182–190 Wairau Road,
Auckland 10, New Zealand

Penguin Books Ltd, Registered Offices:
Harmondsworth, Middlesex, England

First published by Onyx, an imprint of New American Library, a
division of Penguin Putnam Inc.

First Printing, November 2001
10 9 8 7 6 5 4 3 2 1

ONE

There was nowhere to go but up for inmate #7736648367.

Prison is a hellhole for the spirit. It kills some men. Some men it just breaks like a bundle of sticks, leaving them bitter and vengeful. Some men stagger out the door cowed and repentant, while a few exit walking tall, resolved to be better men. On all men, prison leaves its mark. No one who does time locked up in the Gray House escapes without a scar on his soul, a deep humiliating sense of irretrievable loss. A man coming out of prison is never the same man he was going in. It is a sad but unavoidable truth.

There have been one or two exceptions to this rule. And then there are a few people who don't even seem to notice.

* * *

An empty room with a single chair was all he could see when the door opened.

That was what freedom looked like to a man in the midst of hard time.

When a gray-green cement floor, walls, a hard bunk, and iron bars for a view were the circumference of a man's life, that empty room with its single chair looked like blue skies over a distant horizon, with the fragrance of jasmine thrown in.

It looked like hope.

A few right answers. A carefully modulated attitude—part deference, part repentance, part quietly reassuring self-possession—and a man could be a breath away from liberty. Be cool, play it straight, walk—it was a simple formula. It had worked thousands of times. Why not once more?

A guard held the door open for the man to step in. The guard withdrew and closed the door behind him. The man took in the featureless, windowless walls, the hard floor, the harsh fluorescent light. It was a room with all the charm of the principal's office. He was mighty glad to be there.

"Good morning," a voice said.

The prisoner, wearing gray-green state-issue fatigues and a neutral but expectant expression, turned toward the voice at the other end of the room. This prisoner was a tall, disconcertingly good-looking man in the early prime of life, and none of the light appeared to have gone out of his large, liquid dark eyes—the kind of dark eyes women liked to look deep into in the search of truth.

"Good morning," the prisoner said.

"Please state your name for the record."

"Danny Ocean," the prisoner said.

"Thank you," the voice said tonelessly. "You may sit down."

Mr. Danny Ocean glanced back and forth as though presented with a wealth of plush seating choices; then he chose one of the hard, straight-back chairs. He sat and made himself comfortable, looking up genially, thinking, *What a beautiful room: so large and airy.*

"Mr. Ocean, the purpose of this meeting," said a second voice, a woman's, "is to determine whether, if released, you are likely to break the law again."

A purposeful pause.

Danny riffled through the half dozen replies that burst like Poprocks on his tongue, rejecting them all. He waited out the moment, maintaining perfect eye contact.

The female voice went on. "While this was your first conviction, you have been implicated, though never charged, in over a dozen other confidence schemes and frauds. What can you tell us about this?"

"As you say, ma'am," Danny said, "I was never charged." He gave an affable smile to the woman, who had sculpted gray hair with the rigid texture of a helmet and a face just as unmoving.

None of the three members of the parole board—two men in addition to the woman—changed expressions as they stared at Danny from behind the table.

"Mr. Ocean," said another board member, a dour stick of an individual, "what we're trying to find out is, was there a reason you chose to commit this crime, or was there a reason why you simply got caught this time?"

"My wife left me," Danny said, shifting as though uncomfortable at the memory. He gave the smallest shrug. "I was upset. I got into a self-destructive pattern."

"If released," the woman board member said, "is it likely you would fall back into a similar pattern?"

"She already left me once," Danny said. "I don't think she'll do it again just for kicks."

Glances darted among the board members.

"Mr. Ocean," said the third board member, the sternest visaged of the three, "what do you think you would do if released?"

Danny thought deeply. "I don't know," he said, looking from one board member to the others. "How much do you guys make a year?"

They stared at him coldly.

Danny stared back at them, then broke into a congenial grin.

It was a minimum-security prison downstate.

It was not set far back off the road, or distanced from the civilized world with high, razor-wire walls and guard towers bristling with searchlights and automatic firepower. It didn't have body searches and lockdowns for inmate counts twice a day. There was no "hole" or solitary-confinement dungeon.

It wasn't the kind of place where, if you were slightly built, you were destined to become Bruno's girlfriend.

But it was a prison.

You didn't just walk out the door and go up to the races when the ponies were running at Saratoga. You didn't attend your kid's first Little League baseball game. You couldn't take the wife to the latest chick flick she wanted to see at the cineplex. The free ticket your buddy got you for the big game had to go to somebody else. Life stopped.

It was a prison with locked gates, to which someone else had the key.

The day the key turned in the lock and a man could walk out and keep on going was a bright and shining day. No cloud could darken the sun for a man who had finished his time and was once more at blessed liberty. Among all the days in a man's life, he would remember this one most vividly and pleasantly.

"Ocean, Daniel," a guard called out from behind the desk at the prison checkout station.

Danny stepped forth, and the properties clerk doled out the few personal possessions that

Danny had surrendered at the beginning of his term—a watch, a wallet, a wedding ring, a few bills, a plastic bag containing civilian clothes, a pair of shoes, a belt. The guard produced a form on which each item was listed, with a line at the bottom for the former prisoner to certify their return.

"Sign," the guard said, pushing the form in front of Danny.

As Danny snatched up the pen and signed with a flourish—going out was so much easier than coming in—the guard reached down and added a piece of mail to Danny's small pile of possessions. "This came for you today. Rest'll be forwarded to your parole officer."

A second guard, leaning lazily on the counter watching the proceedings, shifted his head a bit to read the return address embossed on the official-looking envelop the properties guard put down. "Those your lawyers?" he drawled with idle interest.

Danny focused on the envelope. "My wife's," he said. He opened the envelope and scanned the documents within. His eyes flickered across the papers, his blank expression hard to read.

"What's it say?" the guard said.

Danny stared at the papers for a beat, then looked up. "I'm a free man," he said and grinned, stuffing the papers in his pocket.

*   *   *

The final staging area for an inmate's first small step into freedom was a changing cubicle the size of an airline john.

Danny shouldered his way in, plucked his folded-up civilian clothes out of the bag, and pulled them on. Pricy slacks, a three-hundred-dollar dress shirt, a thousand-dollar jacket. It was apparent, despite the creases and slight rumple, that there was not a loose thread among them. He tugged his cuffs and smiled; the old skins felt good.

He slipped the cash in the wallet, slid the wallet in his pants. On went the watch. He picked up one last item to put on: a silver wedding band.

Danny considered whether or not he would slide it on.

The lettered brass plaque on the wall outside read:

NEW JERSEY STATE
MINIMUM SECURITY CORRECTIONAL FACILITY

Someone had graffitied below it:

If you were in prison, you'd be home now.

Prison humor from someone who plainly had never done time in prison.

The great metal doors opened, and Danny stood within their frame, ready for release. From a distance he looked good—standing tall, well dressed, a man at ease.

A close observor would pick up the fact that he was indeed wearing his wedding ring. Did it matter? Apparently to Danny, if to no one else.

He hovered there on the threshhold, on the precipice of freedom, for a moment.

The winter wind whistled a little on the far side of the gate, and some trash blew in the street. Danny raised his eyes and took in the scene. The view ahead was not exactly pleasant. Industrial New Jersey—sooty, drab, down-market, dreary. Life was hard out there.

Life inside, however, had barely been life at all.

Danny mustered his courage and took his first step back into free America.

TWO

A summer twilight would have found clamoring, excitement-hungry hoards overrunning the promenade.

Yet at dusk this winter day, the chilly, windblown Atlantic City boardwalk stretched out, nearly empty of people. Here and there along the expanse, a few stalwarts strode the planks, enjoying the blustery ocean air and the crash of the surf. As the frosty night descended, the boardwalk became the exclusive domain of a few hardy deep thinkers who relished the bracing solitude, some couples love was keeping warm, and a sprinkling of the chronically gloomy. No one else would brave the cutting wind that sliced to the bone anyone garbed in anything less than arctic foul-weather gear.

Except . . . one man strolling along in a suit jacket and an open-collar shirt, looking around at all the sights as though it were high summer and a balmy eighty-two degrees.

Danny was out. He was free.

He was back drinking in the inexpensive pleasures of the fully franchised, of any citizen who
enjoyed good standing with the powers that
be—the powers that set the rules by which we all
live . . . or else.

He took one last look around at the sparkling
night and the spacious air and the other pleasures of the unincarcerated and turned in at the
grand entrance of an emporium where nothing
was free.

Coming home for you and me might mean the
hearth and a roaring fire, a comfy chair and a
snifter of brandy. Toss off the shoes, wave the
noisy world good-bye for the nonce, settle in for
some low-sensory-input downtime.

When Danny pushed through the swinging
glass doors and his polished wingtips hit the
plush red carpeting of the Atlantic City Taj
Mahal, every one of his senses lit up like a jackpot. He looked around with a smile that said,
Honey, I'm home.

He sailed into the casino gaming rooms like a
macaw come home to the jungle. The sights. The
sounds. All these gambling natives swirling and
dancing around him. He drank it all in: the buzz
of a casino floor, the hum of conversation, the
ding-ding-ding and *thunk-thunk-thunk* of the slots,
and the delicious brisk whirr and snap of shuffled cards.

Home is where, when you go there, you wonder why you've been elsewhere all this time. There was no question why he was here.

He made his way through the glorious multitude, redolent of sweat, cheap cologne, and cash. He sashayed up to the cashier's window, pulled out his wallet, and extracted several crisp hundreds. Not even noticing the age or gender of the teller behind the cage—too busy taking in the passing parade—he tossed his bills down on the smooth marble and saw them replaced by a neat pile of chips. He swept the chips up; they fell as naturally into his hand as the apple Adam took from Eve.

Ah, the wealth of choices. The cornucopia of pleasures.

He relished the walk back past the roulette pit, eyeballing the poker tables, the Keno lounge, the baccarat games. He circled once and settled down at a blackjack table.

He played a couple of hands, waiting for the old feel to come back.

He craned his neck about the teeming casino, looking for someone—a friend, someone who should be here—but without success. He turned his attention back to his cards and the cards of the dealer.

Nine, ten. Stay. Dealer, seventeen. Danny won.

King, four. Dealer showed a six. Stick. Dealer busted.

Queen, ace. Twenty-one. Danny won again.

Was there any other way? The natural order of things had been restored.

A second dealer relieved the first, and when the new man had completed the handoff and turned toward the players, Danny recognized him with a smile. This joe wasn't the friend he had been scouting for, but two hours out of the joint, any familiar face was welcome.

"Hello, Frank," Danny said.

The new dealer was Frank Catton, and he and Danny went way back at this and other halls.

Frank glanced up at the man who spoke his name, and his eyes went wide, like those of a priest who had discovered he was dealing communion wafers to the devil himself. He quickly hid his astonishment, turning it into puzzlement at a customer's odd mistake.

"I beg your pardon, sir," Frank said. "You must have me confused with someone else. My name is Ramon." He tapped the name embroidered on his vest. "See?"

You are the most African-American-looking Ramon I've ever seen, Danny thought with a wry smile. He was about to continue the dialog when he noticed a pit boss circling close by, glaring at them both. A friend dealing cards to a friend? One of the great no-nos for a casino dealer. A job jeopardizer.

"My mistake," Danny said, standing and collecting his chips—twice as many as when he'd started. "Table's cold anyway."

"You might try the lounge at the Grand, sir," Frank said. "It gets busy around one."

"Thanks," Danny said. He hefted his chips as though he had a fistful of solid-gold doubloons and ambled away without looking back.

He had a few hours to kill. He detoured past one of the three cocktail lounges on the floor to see what kind of talent was keeping the bar stools from floating away.

The lounge at the Grand—the main watering hole back by the baccarat tables—was almost indistinguishable from the main-floor lounge in every other casino on the boardwalk in Atlantic City or, for that matter, in Las Vegas: a U-shaped bar, mirrored walls, banquettes favoring dark reds, small tables with waitresses who came by every thirty seconds with a yen to refill.

Danny tilted up his watch: 12:58. He checked the lounge around him and the adjoining casino floor. A half dozen tired conventioners propped up by the bar, while a blowsy working girl a little past her prime tried to sell them some upstairs entertainment at a group rate.

The gaming room itself was dead. Barely enough gamblers populated the floor to keep the lights on. Prison had more nightlife, Danny thought.

Had the family-friendly-resort concept infected Atlantic City as it had Las Vegas, changing the idea from forbidden fun to good, clean recreation—sending all adults to bed with the

children? he wondered. Whatever happened to
"The lights must never go out. The music must
always play"? Where were all the big kids?

The world had been going to hell in a hand-
basket while he was away for a short couple of
years.

Danny nursed a bourbon and scanned a
folded-back copy of the *New York Times.* His eyes
moved down the page and stopped at a header:

Vegas's Paradiso to Be Razed;
Former Owner Denounces Plans

Two photographs punctuated the article on
the jump on page twelve. The first was of a dark-
eyed, carefully coiffed, expensively suited man
identified as Terry Benedict, a resort developer
and the new owner of the Paradiso Hotel
Casino. He wore a king-of-the-world smile. Par-
tially obscured behind him, clinging to his arm,
was a beautiful woman, definitely of trophy cal-
iber. The second photograph pictured the former
owner of the Paradiso, Reuben Tishkoff, scowling. The pictures pretty much gave the gist of the
story: Somebody was realizing a grand scheme;
somebody else felt he had been hammered in the
process.

Danny studied Terry Benedict's photograph
intently.

"Catching up on current events?" a man's
voice said.

Danny lowered the paper. Sitting across from him was Catton, the blackjack dealer at the Taj, changed out of his dealer's threads.

"Ramon?" Danny said with an arched brow.

"Glad to meet you," Frank said, nodding. "Frank Catton wouldn't get by the gaming board."

Danny already knew that was the reason for the phony name. He knew enough about Frank's history to know that the guy couldn't afford to have it be an open book—especially if the book were to be read by the corporate suits whose worst fear was any whiff of the bad old days when "casino" in America meant "Mob." Any rap sheet whatsoever got you struck from the list of the employable.

"You just get out?" Frank said, giving Danny the once-over.

"This afternoon," Danny said.

"And already turning over a new leaf," Frank chuckled, noting Danny's drink and the environs in which he partook. He signaled a passing waitress; she ignored him. End of her shift. He was invisible.

"You seen him?" Danny said directly. This was why he was here.

"Last I heard he was in LA," Frank said, "teaching movie stars how to play cards." Danny sipped his bourbon, processing that unlikely headline. Frank watched him, a realization dawning. "Why?" he said, after a beat. "You have something planned already?"

"You kidding?" Danny said. "I just became a citizen again." He gazed seriously into the ice at the bottom of his glass as he drained it. He raised his eyes, caught the attention of the bartender, and signaled for a drink for each of them.

Frank stared at Danny until he caught his eye.

Danny looked back at him neutrally, then couldn't help but grin. Of course he had something planned.

Frank turned his eyes to heaven. "Jesus," he said.

Never underestimate the master.

Danny and Frank strolled out to a sub shop on the promenade, thinking about procuring some late-night food. Danny sipped his bourbon and swirled his ice, looking around contentedly like a tourist.

"It's tough now, our line of work," Frank said, studying the all-night menu. "Everybody so serious. Too many guns, too many computers. Whadda you gonna do? Steal from ordinary people?"

"That would be criminal," Danny said. He also studied the menu: not haute cuisine by any stretch; but not prison meatloaf. A plethora of choices.

"So what's left?" Frank said. "Banks? Hah. Banks got no money. It's all electronic. Only place that still takes cash is—"

"Casinos," Danny finished for him. Maybe a

regular meatball sub. Simple, classic. Or a Philly steak. Why not? It had been a while since he'd eaten a decent Philly steak.

"Oh, no," Frank said, realizing the magnitude of the notion, all thoughts of food fleeing his mind.

"Oh, yes," Danny said.

"When?" Frank asked.

"Soon," Danny said. No, meatball it would be. Nothing like an authentic Jersey-Italian meatball sub. "Interested?"

Frank smiled, opened his hands.

Danny had his answer.

They placed their orders with the tall, Mohawk-haired night geek manning the counter. Danny moved over to the pay phone. He pulled a business card from his jacket, picked up the phone, and dialed the number on the card. He waited as it rang.

"Yes, Officer Brooks?" Danny said into the phone. "My name is Danny Ocean. I'm just out. I'm supposed to check in with you within twenty-four hours."

He listened.

"Yes, I know it's late, but I thought I should touch base with you as soon as—"

He listened again.

"No, sir. I haven't gotten into any trouble. No drinking. No, sir."

He tilted his glass and finished his bourbon.

"No, sir. I wouldn't even think of leaving the state."

The sound of a jet flyover punctuated the end of the phone call and the beginning of Danny Ocean's new life. Life after the stir. A new day was dawning for Danny, he knew.

And for Danny's friends.

They just didn't know it yet.

THREE

Los Angeles

The Mondrian was a chic, high-end boutique hotel in West Hollywood where French actresses and British directors and Chech "filmmakers" stayed when they were in town working on a picture—when the money was too obscenely good to keep them at a snob's arm's length across one ocean or another from Hollywood. It was where book agents and magazine editors from New York stayed when they wanted to show they were as hip and in front of the curve as any of the seal-slick studio execs to whom they were trying to peddle their wares.

The hotel was on Sunset Boulevard at the base of the Hollywood Hills, enough up the rise from the flat sprawl of the LA basin that the view from the upper floors was primo. And the view from the penthouse the night of Danny's coming—of the lights of Los Angeles and Santa Monica and the arc of the coast from Malibu down to Palos Verdes, and of the Pacific and Catalina beyond—was such that you'd have sworn you could see Asia had it been daylight.

But who the hell was looking at the view?

Not the gaggle in the smoke-filled penthouse.

Not likely.

A poker game was in progress. Five players, five cigarettes burning in five ashtrays, five tumbler glasses with aged single-malt whiskey, Johnny Walker Black. Hard stuff. You didn't play poker in this crowd and sip a wine spritzer.

In the host chair was a venture-capital high-roller wannabe who had a start-up movie-development company going—small potatoes so far, but they were all his own potatoes. He was a naif among wolves in the movie business, and he knew it—so he was out to remedy the situation. He hung with entertainment types whenever he could, wherever he could, listening, learning, dropping a few bucks if necessary.

Two of the other chairs at the game were warmed by an aging talent agent who knew everybody in the biz all the way back to D. W. Griffith, he claimed, and a filthy-rich independent producer, who for a split second ten years ago had been head of production at Paramount—until he left with a sweetheart deal that his wife and his girlfriend both thought was generous.

Rusty Ryan, in the fourth chair, had been playing for six hours, and he looked tired. Not of the game, but of the players. Rusty was a good-looking guy still on the fair side of thirty. When he wanted to whip it out, he had a smile that would make you believe in friendship. He could sell dirt to a prairie dog if there was a buck fifty at stake. Quick, impatient for the next big thing, he had the attention span of a bee in blossom time.

"That's two hundred to me, is it not?" Rusty said, tossing in chips. "And another two." He added two more. Then he turned to the fifth player—on his left—Kyle Tanner.

Kyle was the baby of the crowd at twenty-two. And better than good-looking. The kid was drop-dead handsome. He knew it. He could be a movie star. In fact, he was. Since he'd been cast from a cattle call on a Cameron Crowe sex-and-sob teens-rule pic when he was sixteen, he'd made an average of two films a year, with bigger and better roles every time. His ego was as big as a house and his bankroll was so fat by now he didn't have the math to count it all.

"Four hundred to me," Kyle said, mulling it over. "Ah, what the hell? Pocket change. Call."

As the betting round continued, Rusty set down his cards and leaned over to Kyle, whispering. "Why you bet a certain way is your business, but you have to make them think you're betting for a reason. Understand?"

Kyle nodded. He was young but not stupid. He had a million-dollar instinct for which scripts to pick, which movies to star in; he had the sense to know that Rusty had a brain full of the kind of know-how a dude in his lofty position should have.

Everybody was in.

Everybody showed 'em.

Kyle cased the hands: mostly junk. Until he got to Rusty's. Full house, kings over fours.

"You the man, Rusty," Kyle said with a big smile.

Rusty nodded—at this table, of course he was.

He rose. "Rake that in for me," he said, then walked in the direction of the bathroom in the master bedroom.

While Rusty peed out some twelve-year-old scotch, washed his hands, and doused his cheeks with cold water, somebody new was approaching the penthouse. This man came out of the elevator, crossed to the door of the suite, and knocked on the mahogany door. By the time Rusty had stared at his fatigued eyes in the mirror, combed his hair with his fingers, checked his fly, and wandered back to the table, there was a sixth man in the room.

As Rusty walked back in the room from the john, he looked the newcomer over carefully, assessing his potential.

"Hey, Rusty," Kyle said, "we got another player if that's all right."

Danny Ocean nodded. Gave a half smile all around. "I hope this isn't an intrusion," he said, discreetly slipping a money clip from one hand to the other. "The concierge mentioned there was a game in progress."

On Rusty, the money clip was not lost. This guy had come to play. "No intrusion at all," he said. "I'm Rusty Ryan."

"Danny Ocean," Danny said.

Everybody else at the table had eagerly taken note of the money clip. Fresh meat.

Danny shook hands with Rusty, then with those seated around the table. He found a chair, and bought a more than respectable stake from the kitty. Everybody was smiling a welcome for the new guy.

The game began anew. Rusty anted up. "If you don't mind my asking, what do you do, Mr. Ocean?" Rusty said.

"I'm in finance," Danny said. He threw some chips into the center of the table and took some cards.

"Sounds interesting," Rusty said.

"Not really," Danny said. "Just a matter of moving money from one place to another."

"Keeps you busy?" Rusty said.

Danny shrugged. He cocked his head and assessed his cards.

The other players studied him out of the corners of their eyes as they computed the odds in this particular round. Not good, in the estimation of two combatants. They both folded.

Kyle picked at his cards, scanned them, reordered them, while debating internally.

Rusty finally leaned in. "Kyle," he said, low,

"you know what you have. Looking at them doesn't change them. Leave 'em where they are and make your bet."

"Right," Kyle said. "One thousand. Okay."

"Your five," Danny said, "and another fifteen." He then looked up at Rusty, picking up their interrupted conversation. "You?" he said.

Standard conversational rhythm, card-game style.

"At the moment," Rusty said, "I seem to have found a home in the entertainment industry. Isn't that right, Kyle?"

Kyle flipped him an acknowledging grin. Rusty Ryan, card guru to the stars. A respectable and hardly new Hollywood calling. Pros in golf, tennis, polo, sailing—pros with a passel of patience and a little bit of hustle in their souls— had long been able to make a decent living catering to indecently rich show-biz types— parvenus hungry for the cosmopolitan skills of the wellborn.

"Your fifteen," Rusty said to Danny, "and fifteen more."

"Three to me, right?" Kyle said.

Kyle started to check his cards again, but remembered Rusty's admonishment and threw his chips in.

Danny, on the other hand, gave his hand a glance. "Contrary to what Mr. Ryan may say, Kyle," Danny said, "I check my cards before I make a bet." He gave Kyle a thin smile. "But be careful," he said after a pause. "I can tell from your face you're holding three of a kind."

Kyle's eyes grew wide.

"Fifteen," Danny said, pushing more chips in, "and another three."

Danny and Rusty were now staring each other down. No love lost between them. This new cat was messing with Rusty's meal ticket.

Finally, Rusty smiled coldly and dropped his cards. "Out," he said.

Kyle pursed his lips and stared at the pot. It was just him and Danny now. He was out there in the deep water without a lifeboat. He wanted to look at Rusty for a clue, but knew what a dork he would appear to be. "Three grand," he breathed. "Three grand."

"If you've got to do it, do it, Kyle," Rusty said, his eyes fixed on Danny in a none-too-friendly stare.

"He can make up his own mind," Danny said softly.

"He's bluffing," Rusty said.

"There's only one way to know," Danny said, his hands folded over his cards on the table.

Kyle considered the pot. He felt Rusty silently urging him on.

"Okay, okay," Kyle said, throwing in the bet. "Call."

Danny lifted his hands and turned the cards over. Four nines.

Kyle's face dropped. He tossed in his cards

and took a deep breath. Pocket change that pot wasn't.

For the first time in the game, Rusty blanched. "Shit," he said quietly. "I really thought he was bluffing. Sorry, Kyle."

Danny raked in the pot, quite a large pile of chips. The hand was definitely an evening ender.

Danny stood and walked around the table to convert his winnings to cash. "Thanks for the game," he said, nodding to Kyle. "By the way, I'm a big fan of your work."

Rusty and the four other players watched him walk out the door with their money.

Sayonara.

Rusty's Mercedes swept along Sunset Boulevard through opulent residential sections—Beverly Hills, Westwood, Bel Air. Light nighttime traffic. There was zero smog, an offshore marine breeze having flushed the western basin, leaving behind something cool and fresh to breathe.

Rusty and Danny rode silently, staring out opposite windows at the lighted estates set back on blue-green lawns.

No actual human beings were about. Certainly nobody walking—heck, there were no sidewalks. Just the residential ziggurats of those lucky few who knew the great secret of amassing wealth in this well-watered desert.

Is there an agenda here? Rusty thought, giving Danny a sidelong glance. *Or is this just a good-old-boy college reunion? Well, let's find out.*

"God, I'm bored," Rusty said.

"You look bored," Danny said.

"I'm so bored," Rusty said. "That kind of thing is just . . . unprofessional. Kid actors. They pay someone to exercise with 'em. They pay someone to tell 'em what to eat. They pay me to play cards with 'em."

Danny smiled to himself. He didn't have to lay any groundwork, no need to lay it on, reel his fish in slowly. He didn't have to say a word. Rusty was doing it all for him.

"How was the clink?" Rusty asked. "You get the cookies I sent you?"

"Why do you think I came to see you first?" Danny said. He reached in his jacket pocket and pulled out a wad of bills—the take from the Mondrian game. He peeled off half and handed them across to Rusty. "Six grand," Danny said. "Half of it's yours."

"There has to be something better than this," Rusty said, pocketing the loot without even looking at it. Rusty had been hustling cards at the pro level since he was sixteen. At seventeen—passing as twenty-one—he got eighty-sixed from all the casinos in New Jersey for counting cards. Now he couldn't enter a casino in America under his own name. "Tell me you've got something better than this," he said.

"I've got something better than this," Danny said.

*   *   *

Canter's Deli in Hollywood catered to working comics, old movie bit players, young starv-
ing actors, screenwriters between jobs, and
neighborhood kvetchers and kibbitzers from the
surrounding Fairfax shtetl. Day and night it was
populated by a shifting cross section of industry
haves and have-nots, loyal in fat times and thin.
It had a big menu and huge sandwiches. It was
the closest thing to an authentic New York Jew-
ish deli this side of the Hudson River. A few
years back the old place had been renovated to
keep pace with changing times. It ended up
looking even more retro fifties than before. The
booths were still sticky and the sandwiches were
the same XL size. Everybody was happy.

Danny and Rusty sat in a booth in the side
room over coffee, where it was not so crowded.
Not the retired-comedians-outyelling-each-other
room, not the room where they shot the famous
feigned-orgasm/I'll-have-what-she's-having
scene from *When Harry Met Sally*.

"How's Tess?" Rusty said.

Danny stared at him. Next subject, please.

"All right," Rusty said. He sipped a little coffee. "Tell me."

"It's tricky," Danny said, and he sipped a little
coffee also. "No one's ever done it before. Needs
planning, a large crew."

"Guns?" Rusty said, holding up his steaming
mug.

"Not loaded ones," Danny said. "It has to be

very precise. There's a lot of security. But the take . . ."

"What's the target?" Rusty said.

Not finished with the sell, Danny went on. ". . . eight figures each."

"What's. The. Target?" Rusty said pointedly.

Danny took a deep breath. "When's the last time you were in Vegas?" he said.

"What?" Rusty said with a hiss. "You wanna knock over a casino?"

Danny put down his coffee, shook his head, and lifted three fingers.

Rusty had to put down his mug too. He looked hard at Danny. Then he shifted his gaze out the window at the night people walking by on Fairfax—more or less normal people, all of them—dreamers, too, probably. But sane.

FOUR

Downtown Los Angeles was not what outsiders thought of when they thought of the city of Los Angeles.

Seen from everywhere else in the sprawling, sun-blasted basin popularly known as LA, "downtown" thrust up like the city of Oz in the distance, an isolated shimmer of office towers in the east. Remote. Far inland from the ocean and its cooling breezes. Different from the bungalow-and-palm-tree profile of West LA. Maybe a little foreign to Westsiders, who almost never had reason to go down there.

But it was real all right—a furious dynamo of commerce during the workday, a Pacific Rim juggernaut powered by international trade and shipping, big-dollar real-estate deal brokering, lawyering on a gigantic scale, old-fashioned newspapering, the small, constant whirr of garment making.

In the daytime, downtown rocked. The Hong Kong of the occident.

At night, it was an eerie, depleted, post-neutron-bomb locale—echoing, hollowed out. Dark and dead. The towers loomed, the traffic lights flashed red and green, late commuters sped out of underground garages and disappeared west and east.

The streets, in the midst of this gargantuan construct of human industry and wealth, were abandoned.

Prowl cars cruised slowly, protecting the lair of the coastal Mammon.

The wealth was safe. The means of creating it, matrixed in the gleaming towers, were secure. It would take an army to extract it from these high-tech high-rises.

On the fortieth floor of the swank new Library Tower building, in the cossetted heart of downtown, two people walked the dark corridors of one high-hat establishment.

Predators.

Hunters seeking a key to unlock the wealth buried in the matrix.

Their flashlight beams strafed the interior of the elegant, wood-paneled offices. Engraved brass on the beveled-glass-inlaid exterior doors announced J. A. Kuehn & Associates, Architects.

Danny and Rusty were doing some late-night reconnaissance. As Danny pawed through a cabinet full of blueprints, Rusty passed the time switching papers from a desk's IN box to its OUT box.

At last, Danny found the right set of blueprints and draped them across a desk. He scanned the master drawing, then flipped it back, thumbing through subsets until he found the key he was looking for.

The blueprint of his dreams. The dreams of a thousand nights in stir while the plan took shape.

The blueprint was made up of myriad lines, angles, arcs, dimensions. It might as well have been the Pyramid at Giza, to the untutored eye. Rusty peered over his shoulder, clueless to what he was seeing.

"The vault at the Bellagio," Danny said.

And magically the blueprint coalesced into rational shape and form for Rusty. Walls, doors, bulkheads, hallways. His heart leapt. There it was, all laid out so prettily. He scanned the document, grinning. He shifted it over and peered at the plans underneath it: a cross section on the vertical.

Rusty's heart fell.

"If I'm reading this right," he said, "and I think I am, this is probably the least accessible vault ever designed." He zeroed in and really studied the blueprint. "Oops," he said. "Actually, you know what? I'm wrong. It's *definitely* the least accessible vault ever designed."

"Yep," Danny said.

Rusty's brow furrowed a little. "You said three

casinos." He looked up, holding out hope that the other two would be more feasible.

No such luck.

"These," Danny said, pointing to angled passageways, "feed into the cashier cages at both the Mirage and the MGM Grand."

He flipped to the next blueprint.

"But every dime ends up here," he said, tapping the main vault.

"The Bellagio, the Mirage, and the MGM. Those are Terry Benedict's places," Rusty said.

"Yes, they are," Danny said. "Think he'll mind?"

"More than somewhat," Rusty said. He began to smile despite himself.

Outside the architectural firm's suite, at the bank of elevators facing the elegant beveled glass doors of J. A. Kuehn & Associates, a light flashed over one of the elevators. No ding of arrival, just a silent light. The elevator doors slid open to reveal a security guard within. He was there to make his nightly tour. A large fellow, he had to duck to exit the elevator car. He crossed the hallway and checked the doors to the architecture firm.

Locked.

He riffled through his electronic key cards and found the right one. He slipped it in the slot and pushed the ornate brass handle down. . . .

*   *   *

Danny and Rusty leisurely reassembled the set of blueprints while they talked. Danny rolled the documents up and carefully slotted them back into the rack in the cabinet where he'd found them.

Rusty considered the plan that Danny had just laid out.

"You'd need at least a dozen guys," he said, "doing a combination of cons."

"Like what?" Danny said. This was why he wanted Rusty. He'd been waiting months—years—to hear his take.

"Well," Rusty said, "off the top of my head, I'd say you're looking at a Boesky, a Jim Brown, a Miss Daisy, two Jethros, and a Leon Spinks. Oh, and the biggest Ella Fitzgerald ever."

Perfect. Almost exactly what Danny had been thinking. They were on the same page. Nothing like working with a pro. Danny swung the blueprint cabinet door shut and pushed it until the latch clicked.

"Where do you think you're gonna get the money to back this?" Rusty asked.

"As long as we're hitting these three casinos, we'll get our bankroll," Danny said. "Terry Benedict has a list of enemies."

"But does he have enemies with loose cash and nothing to lose?" Rusty said. Then he smiled as the light dawned. "Aha," he said.

"Aha," Danny said, smiling also.

"Rueben," Rusty said.

Rueben Tishkoff, former owner of the Las

Vegas Paradiso Hotel Casino. As last pictured in the *New York Times*, scowling foully, next to a picture of the new owner, Terry Benedict, who was smiling broadly.

The oversize security guard moved silently through the suite, listening, homing in on what was an unusual sound for that time of night—voices. He passed a receptionist's desk, turned down a hallway, and stealthily made his way forward.

"So," Rusty was saying, as they tidied up the desk they'd been using, "here's what I think. You should take this plan, kick it around for a week or two. Sleep on it. Turn it over in your head. Then *never bring it up to me again*."

He was flat serious.

"Uh-huh," Danny said. "So what are you saying?"

Rusty rolled his eyes. "I'm saying this is like trying to build a house of cards on the deck of a speeding boat."

"Really?" Danny said. "I thought it was much harder than that."

Suddenly, the security guard's flashlight beam hit them square in the eyes. Danny and Rusty put their hands up to block the light.

"Jesus, Oscar, lower it a little, will ya?" Danny said.

"Sorry," the security guard said, lowering his beam. "You two done up here? Find what you wanted?"

"Yeah, thanks," Danny said. "You mind if we borrow a couple drawings for the night? Make some copies."

"Whatever you need," the security guard said.

Danny withdrew his money clip, peeled off a couple hundreds, and buried them in the security guard's hand.

"'Preciate it," Danny said.

Danny and Rusty waited for a car at the fortieth floor elevator bay, each lost in his own thoughts. When the elevator door finally opened, Rusty stopped Danny from boarding.

"I need a reason," he said. "And don't say money. Why do this?"

"Why not do it?" Danny said matter-of-factly.

Rusty tried to stare him down—enough bullshitting around.

"Because yesterday I walked out of the joint wearing my entire wardrobe and you're cold-decking *TeenBeat* coverboys," Danny said.

Meaningful pause.

"Because the house always wins," he continued. "You play long enough, never changing stakes, the house takes you."

Second meaningful pause.

"Unless when that special hand comes around," he said, "you bet big. And then you take the house."

Rusty smiled. "You've been practicing that speech, haven't you?" he said.

"A little," Danny said, deadpan. "Did I rush it? It felt like I rushed it."

"No," Rusty said, "it was good."

They stepped aboard the elevator. As the door closed, Rusty said, "I wonder what Reuben will say?"

Danny and Rusty looked at each other.

"You're out of your goddamn minds," they mimicked simultaneously.

FIVE

Las Vegas

"**Y**ou're *out* of your goddamn *minds!*" Reuben Tishkoff barked at them over scotch in his opulent backyard in the furnace-hot Vegas afternoon heat.

Almost perfect, but they'd gotten the inflection a little off. Reuben never was completely predictable. It was what made him a tough nut in any business transaction.

Reuben carried, forever cemented on his face, the grimace of a man in harried midmovement. Maybe it was the high-stakes nature of the casino racket. Maybe it was the constant heat and desert dust in the Las Vegas air. You could always see his brain working in his face.

He scrutinized his two lunch guests at poolside. "Are you listening to me?" he said. "You are, both of you, nuts." He looked from one to the other. "I know more about casino security

than any man alive. I invented it, and it cannot
be beaten. They got cameras, they got watchers,
they got locks, they got timers, they got vaults.
They got enough armed personnel to occupy
Paris. Okay, bad example."

"It's never been tried," Danny said.

"Oh, it's been tried," Tishkoff said. "A few
guys even came close. You know the three most
successful robberies in Vegas history?"

Danny and Rusty did not know, but even if
they did, they knew enough to let Reuben spiel
out the stories. Although they were negative stories that they'd prefer not to hear. Especially if
the stories were true, as these probably would
be.

Reuben leaned forward and spieled, poking
the air with his fork. "The Sands Casino. 1965,"
he said. "Number three, the bronze medal. Pencil neck grabs a lockbox at the Sands. Guy
looked just like Adlai Stevenson, came up behind a carrier and snatched the box. He took almost three steps before five security men hit
him. They got it on the security cameras—the
look of horror on the guy's face. It must be like
what NFL quarterbacks go through every Sunday. Five guys leapt on him at once. He got two
steps closer to the door than any living soul before him."

Reuben took a forkful of salad to let the story
sink in. He jabbed the air again. "The Flamingo.
Casino floor. 1971," he said. "Second most successful robbery. A hippie grabbed a tray full of

chips and raced toward the electronic sliding doors. This guy actually smelled fresh oxygen before they got him. As the doors began to part, *whap!* a billy club comes outta nowhere. Across his skull. It was Chicago '68 all over again. He was breathing out of a hose the next three weeks, goddamn hippie."

Danny and Rusty listened politely. It was all part of the process. Reuben Tishkoff had been around the block in Vegas before they'd even had blocks. He deserved proper respect.

"And the closest any man has gotten to robbing a Las Vegas casino," Tishkoff said, "was Caesar's Palace. 1987. This Euro wank made a grab and actually got out the door. Took five steps—the tourists and valets scattering for their lives—and the glass explodes from three different doors behind him and he arches his back in agony. They got pictures of that, too. He came, he grabbed, they conquered. Bullets ripped the putz to shreds. Ended up on Caesar's steps a bloody pulp."

Rusty and Danny forked in a little salad and took hits on their cocktails, dutifully looking as though they were absorbing the full cautionary seriousness of the homilies.

"But what am I saying?" Tishkoff said, changing tone as though just realizing to whom he was talking. "You guys are pros, the best. I'm sure you can make it out of the casino. Of course, lest we forget, once you're out the front door, you're still in the middle of the fucking desert!"

Both Danny and Rusty made their best effort to look chastened.

"You're right," Rusty said. "He's right," Rusty said to Danny.

"Reuben, you're right," Danny said. "Our eyes are bigger than our stomachs."

"That's exactly it," Rusty said. "Pure ego."

"Yeah, yeah, blah, blah," Tishkoff said, suspicious. They were giving up way too easily. He was missing something. He was being set up. He could feel it.

"Thank you so much for setting us straight," Danny said. "Sorry we bothered you."

They both rose to go.

Definitely a setup, Tishkoff thought, also rising. These mooks were holding back big-time— something they weren't telling him. He knew how guys like this thought. "Look, we go all the way back," he said, smiling. "I owe you from that thing with the guy in the place, and I'll never forget it."

"It was our pleasure," Danny said.

"I'd never been to Belize," Rusty said.

They all smiled some more, exchanging handshakes, back pats. Danny and Rusty turned again to go, turned toward Reuben's grand, lushly landscaped villa that said the man had definitely been a player in this brutal, rattler-infested desert oasis.

"Give Dominic your addresses," Tishkoff said. "I got some remaindered furniture I wanna send you."

Danny and Rusty smiled, waved over their shoulders, and began to circle the pool to leave. Tishkoff, of course, wouldn't let them go that easily. He just couldn't.

"Just out of curiosity," he said, "which casinos did you geniuses pick to rob?"

Danny stopped, almost as if he had been waiting for this question, which of course he had.

"The Bellagio, the Mirage, and the MGM Grand," Danny said.

"Those are Terry Benedict's casinos," Tishkoff said. His nostrils flared, smelling a rat.

"Say, you know, he's right," Rusty said, as if realizing the fact for the first time.

Tishkoff swirled the ice in his drink, then waved them back. "You guys," he said with his grimacing smile. "Whadda you got against Terry Benedict?"

"What do *you* have against him?" Danny said. "That's the real question."

"He torpedoed my casino, muscled me out," Tishkoff said. "Now he's gonna blow it up next month to make way for another eyesore. Don't think I don't see what you're doin'."

"What are we doing, Reuben?" Rusty said innocently.

"You gonna steal from Terry Benedict," Tishkoff said, "you better goddamn know how. This sorta thing used to be civilized. You'd hit a guy, he'd whack you. Done. But Benedict . . ." Tishkoff bristled.

Danny and Rusty watched him closely. It was going along just as they'd hoped. Looking good.

"At the end of this he better not know you're involved," Tishkoff said. "He'd better not know your names or he'd better think you're dead because he'll kill you, and *then* he'll go to work on you."

"That's why we've got to be very careful," Danny said. "We have to be precise. We have to be well-funded."

"Yeah, you gotta be nuts too," said Tishkoff. "And you're gonna need a crew as nuts as you are."

After a pregnant silence, Tishkoff said, "Who do you have in mind?"

Danny and Rusty both smiled; they'd hooked their fish.

And so it began. . . .

SIX

Los Angeles

"All right," Rusty said, "who's in?"

"Frank C. is in," Danny said.

They were sitting at a cafe on the Venice Beach boardwalk, back in LA, far enough up the strand from the ridiculous Muscle Beach weight-lifting pen so they wouldn't have to be embarrassed by other people's sweaty exertions.

They compared their lists, scribbled on pieces of hotel stationery.

"Frank C. developed a bad case of bronchitis," Danny said. "He put in for a transfer to warmer climates."

Frank Catton had described to Danny his regretful resignation from his Atlantic City casino job—coughing disgustingly on his boss's desk, spitting into a handkerchief, as the man filled out paperwork.

"Frank's already feeling better," Danny said.

*   *   *

As they spoke, Frank was deplaning at Mc-Carran International Airport in Las Vegas. He strode into the baggage area, grabbed his suitcase and garment bag from the carousel, and exited into the salubrious Vegas sun.

Under a WELCOME TO LAS VEGAS banner, he stopped, put his bags down, and lit a cigarette. He inhaled with deep satisfaction, his apparent bronchitis miraculously cured.

He moved on toward the taxi bay.

"What about drivers?" Danny said, watching the in-line skaters in their sway-top bikinis roll by on the Venice bike path.

Rusty was tracking a pair of blondes with X-rated bodies receding in a southerly direction. "I talked to the Malloys yesterday," he said.

"The Mormon twins?" Danny said, his attention wandering in the same direction.

"They're both in Salt Lake City," Rusty said.

At a vacant, weedy drag racetrack in Salt Lake City, two souped-up tractor-wheeled monster trucks, their engines roaring before a starting line, were itching to leap across it and go.

The first monster truck, its engine revving loudly, howled and trembled and made little reflexive jerks toward the line.

Next to this was an infinitely larger, souped-up, belching monster truck—an actual, life-size truck.

The first one, sprouting an antenna from its back bumper, was a micromonster—a remote-control toy standing just a foot and a half off the ground.

The engines roared, each one at a pitch appropriate to its size, both vibrating vehicles aimed down the track at the same finish line a hundred yards away. This was a genuine, side-by-side race.

The drivers stared each other down: Turk Malloy, six feet up in the cab of the real truck; and Virgil Malloy, feet on the ground trackside, remote control in his hands.

"They're nice boys, the Malloys," Danny said. "Really."

"They're six months off the job," Rusty said.

Lights flashed red to yellow to green at the drag racetrack, and the big truck coated the asphalt with rubber, gained traction, and grabbed the early lead.

Virgil's toy spun its wheels, fishtailed, and got off to an agonizingly slow start.

But as the big truck bellowed down the track, the little truck came zipping up fast, headed for the front and a sure win. It was looking to be an embarrassment for Turk, until he jerked his wheel a little and—*ka-thunk!*—flattened his brother's radio-controlled vehicle.

Virgil pouted as he plucked the smoking wreckage of his entry off the track.

*   *   *

"I got the sense," Rusty said, "they're having trouble filling the hours."

Danny nodded, watching a stoner sit down at the edge of the boardwalk and light up a joint. Two Britney Spears look-alikes picked up the aroma in passing and sat down beside him and shared.

Danny went back to his list. "Electronics?" he said.

"Livingston Dell," Rusty said. "Livingston's been doing freelance surveillance work of late for the FBI Mob Squad," Rusty said.

In San Diego, two mobsters on a meet in a public park peered over their shoulders, making certain no one was watching them.

Little did they know. . . .

Livingston Dell, anorexic audio-visual junkie and victim of a continual flop sweat, crouched before the mobsters' pixilated image on a black-and-white monitor inside a surveillance van, masterfully controlling his surveillance camera with a joystick in his hand.

He was flanked by FBI men, one of whom reached over to adjust a monitor.

"D-Don't . . . touch . . . it," Livingston stammered.

"What?" the first FBI man said.

Livingston turned on him testily. "Do you see me pulling the gun out of your holster and firing it?"

"Hey, Radio Shack, relax," the FBI man said.

*   *   *

"How are Livingston's nerves?" Danny said.

Danny and Rusty shielded their papers, pulling them back out of sight as the cut, buff, macho waiter put down their espressos.

"Okay," said Rusty. "Not so bad you'd notice."

"*Autre choses?*" said the waiter in decidedly queenie French. "Anything else?"

Danny and Rusty stared at him until he flounced away. They both raised their pinkies and sipped.

An undercover cop in jeans and a T-shirt sat down next to the stoner and the two Britneys on the Venice boardwalk and asked for a toke.

Rusty and Danny watched.

The stoner passed the narc the joint. The cop sniffed it and signaled by raising it in the air. Two uniformed cops came up and arrested the kids. The crowd hissed and pointed as the narcs led the kids away. Then the people went back to their skateboarding and henna body painting and navel piercing.

Rusty and Danny got back to business.

"Munitions," Rusty said, checking off the next item on his list.

"Phil Turentine," Danny said.

"Dead," Rusty said.

"No shit?" Danny said. "On the job?"

"Sun cancer," Rusty answered.

"You send flowers?" Danny asked.

"Dated his wife a while," Rusty said.

Danny took that in. Sad news. He sipped his espresso, spending the next few moments in silent memorial to Phil and his many professional accomplishments. Not the least of which was the Fourth of July when he personally took out the Philadelphia Main Line. Phil had hooked up with the famous B & E father-and-son team of Dick and Kelly Boyd. Phil, who prided himself in using a different m.o. every time out, fitted Kelly's five-foot-wingspan, radio-controlled model Cessna with a small shaped charge in the nose. He destroyed a key relay switch ninety feet up on a high-tension tower, disabling burglar alarms to over forty mansions and estates, half of which were empty and ripe for the picking. It looked like a freak accident, so no alert went out. Dick and Kelly took their time and harvested a golden crop.

"Basher," Danny said, moving onto the next candidate.

"We may be too late," Rusty said, checking his watch. "He's on a job. And I know the guys running it." He shook his head with misgiving, signaling for the check. They had to move quickly.

It was Sunday. Banks were closed all day Sunday, making it Basher Tarr's one regular workday of the week.

A pair of goggles over his eyes reflected a

match being struck, then touched to a fuse. "Sweet," Basher said. High praise from an explosives expert, if he did say so himself.

Bang!

Wood shards and splinters of glass flew all around. Basher merely ducked his head and whistled. As the dust settled, three men moved quickly past Basher and into what the settling smoke and dust revealed to be a dynamited bank vault.

A perfect blow. Minimum firepower, maximum return. A single charge and the vault door hung at an angle, sprung wide enough for the men to move in and out without having to touch a thing. The work of a true pro.

There was one little problem though.

Alarms began to sound.

This was news of the worst kind.

Basher was openmouthed with disbelief. "You know, you guys had one job to do," he complained to the rest of his gang, his temper flaring.

He was kicking himself up and down the block for working with vapor-headed amateurs as he exited through the front doors with the rest of the bad-news crew, their hands over their heads. Uniformed cops and SWAT members circled the group, with weapons trained on them, barking a stream of instructions.

Basher got handcuffed behind his back and was seated in the open back door of a squad car, his feet on the pavement. An explosives cop kneeled in front of him, examining his clothing, his pant legs, his shirtsleeves, without touching them.

"And that's all you used during the event?" the cop asked. "Nothing else?"

"Are you accusing me of booby-trapping?" Basher said.

"Well, how 'bout it?" the cop said.

"Booby traps aren't Mr. Tarr's style," a voice said from behind the cop.

The cop turned. Standing behind him, stone-faced, was Rusty, in a dark suit and shades. "Isn't that right, Basher?" Rusty said.

"That's right," Basher said.

"Peck, ATF," Rusty announced, flashing a badge briefly. He addressed the cop. "Let me venture a guess. A simple G4 mainliner, double coil, back wound, quick fuse with a drag under twenty feet."

The explosives cop nodded, impressed.

"That's our man," Rusty said. "Tell me something else. Have you checked him for booby traps on his person? I mean really checked, not just the obvious."

The cop looked bewildered. Rusty stepped forward, yanked Basher to his feet, and spun him around. He moved his hands up and down Basher's legs, around his waist, under his arms.

"Will you go find Griggs and tell him I need to see him?" Rusty said.

"Who?" the cop said.

"Just go find him, will you?" Rusty said loudly, annoyed.

Confused, the cop stalked off, looking for his commanding officer.

"How fast can you put something together with what I just passed you?" Rusty said under his breath.

"Done," Basher said. "Thirty seconds all right?"

"From when?" Rusty said.

"Now," Basher said, snapping something behind his back.

Rusty and Basher were on the move, hurrying. Ahead of them were a wall of squad cars, a police cordon, and a crowd of onlookers.

"Ten seconds?" Rusty said.

"Not quite," Basher said. "Is Danny here?"

"Around the corner," Rusty said.

"Be good working with professionals again," Basher said.

"Okay—go!" Basher said, timing the move.

They both started running.

"Everyone down!" Rusty shouted. "Get down! There's a bomb in the—"

Behind them, the squad car erupted with a deafening roar.

A collective scream rose from the crowd, everyone ducked, cops hit the ground and covered their heads. Onlookers scattered with cries of fright, dragging their children to safety.

Rusty and Basher jogged briskly past the cops,

dodging their splayed legs like tires on an obstacle course.

By the time the explosives cop thought to look around for Basher, both he and Agent Peck, ATF, had disappeared.

SEVEN

Santa Monica

Not since he was a kid in Redbank, New Jersey, had Danny been in a real big top, a real circus tent. He'd hated it then—the heat, the smells, the phony drama, the overhyped, undertalented acts, not to mention the claustrophobia—and he hated it now.

Ringling Brothers, however, this was not.

To begin with, there were no smells.

Second, it was an air-conditioned tent.

Third, a constant whirl of activity with no phony barker announcing the Second Coming of Christ in tights.

The Chinese National Circus was touring the western United States with its troop of elegant trapeze artists, gymnastic teams, and trampoline daredevils. They swung, somersaulted, spun, and flew through the air with a finesse that made the Flying Wallendas look awkwardly earthbound.

A full house applauded every precision-timed feat.

Danny and Rusty, tough guys in Toyland, sat in the bleachers, surrounded by parents and kids munching on spindles of cotton candy.

"Ladies and gentlemen, the Amazing Yen!" an announcer said in Chinese, then repeated it in English.

Yen began his high-wire act.

"Technically," Rusty said, "he's a funambulist. And he is amazing."

"So he can walk on a rope," Danny said, unimpressed.

"More than that," Rusty said.

"So he can juggle," Danny said. "We need a grease man, not an acrobat. Who else is on the list?"

"He is the list," Rusty said.

"Who else?" Danny said, rejecting the notion outright.

"Watch," Rusty said.

Halfway across the wire, Yen the Funambulist sat. And very slowly, but without hesitation, he contorted himself into a ball, never losing his balance. A small, tidy, compact ball on a thin wire.

Even Danny was impressed.

"That's your grease man," Rusty said.

In the blink of an eye, Yen rolled out of his little ball and was again fully upright, a lithe young Chinese man walking the wire.

*   *   *

Danny and Rusty exited the circus tent and walked the length of the Santa Monica pier toward the parking lot, headed for their car.

Yen had been a surprise, Danny thought, a pleasant one. New young blood. Sharp eyes, fast reactions, an acutely developed sense of professionalism. Exactly what they needed.

Why Saul came to his mind just then, he couldn't say.

"We need Saul," Danny said.

"He won't come," Rusty replied. "He swore off the game a year ago."

"He get religion?" Danny asked.

"Ulcers," Rusty said.

"You can ask him," Danny said.

Rusty stopped, stared at Danny, and sighed resignedly. "I can ask," he said.

It was a long trip for a quick no, Rusty thought, getting off the plane in Miami.

True, they needed Saul, needed his gravitas, his presence—or at least the presence he used to have. When healthy and in his prime, Saul could enter a room and take up all the space. The steam went out of other people's conversations within a twenty-foot radius as he filled out the role of international financier, or oil mogul, or South African diamond merchant—or whatever the scam called for.

Rusty walked out of the terminal into the suffocating heat and humidity of southern Florida. So uncomfortable was he, after the desert-dry heat of Vegas and LA, that he was sure mildew was growing on his face as he made his way to the taxi bay. He wiped his face with a handkerchief as he climbed into a blessedly air-conditioned taxi.

"The dogs," he said to the driver. That was all he needed to say. The dog track was Saul's "office." You want to find the butterfly? Go to where the daisies grow.

The patron at the betting window at the track seemed a little befuddled; certainly he seemed older than his fifty years.

Saul Bloom, dressed in a corduroy jacket patched at the elbows and a duffer's hat, fumbled a bit with his money as he counted it out, his mind plainly not on the task at hand. He pushed the cash through the window to the betting clerk, listing off his bets one by one. When the tickets came back to him in a bunch, he came into sharp focus for an instant as he checked the numbers; then he plunged them into his pants pocket and ambled away again in a fuzz.

Rusty, looking as dapper as Saul was down-at-the-heel, stood in the track lobby behind a pillar watching the man do his business. Saul's appearance didn't bother him; he'd seen the transformation that came over him on jobs several times before. That was what made a good con: the ability to morph when the chips were down. Saul had it. That wasn't the problem.

The problem was that the kryptonite in his

belly—the ulcer—had apparently made Saul forget his special powers.

When Saul disappeared into the tunnel leading back to the track, Rusty moved.

Saul plopped down in the cheaper seats in the infield, sitting on one of the long, general admission steps under the box seats. He produced an orange from his pocket and started to peel it. And stopped.

A pair of well-shined shoes appeared behind him. Saul sensed their presence, but didn't turn around. He didn't need to.

"I saw you in the paddock before the second race, outside the men's room, when I placed my bet," Saul said. "I saw you before you even got up this morning."

"How ya been, Saul?" Rusty asked.

"Never better," Saul said.

"What's with the orange?"

"My doctor says I need vitamins."

"So why don't you take vitamins?" Rusty said.

For the first time, Saul craned his neck and shot a look up at Rusty, his eyes suddenly sharp and flinty. "You here to give me a physical?" he said.

"I got a box seat," Rusty said. "Come on."

A waiter came up the steps and served Cuban coffee to Rusty and Saul in the roped-off, plush-chaired box seat.

"I thought you drank Bloody Marys at the track, Saul," Rusty said.

"A man shouldn't drink on the job," Saul said.

He's grumpy, thought Rusty. *Suspicious. Saul hasn't mellowed at all.*

"Who we rooting for here?" Rusty said, indicating the dogs ready in the starting gate.

"Number four," Saul said.

The bell sounded. The electronic rabbit was released and the dogs broke out of the gate. From this point Saul's eyes never left the race. "You gonna ask me," he said, tracking his dog with binoculars, "or should I just say no and get it over with?"

"Saul," Rusty said, "you're the best there is. You're in Cooperstown. What do you want?"

"Nothin'," Saul said. "I got a duplex now. I got wall-to-wall and a goldfish. I'm seeing a nice lady who works the unmentionables counter at Macy's. I've changed."

"Guys like us don't change, Saul," Rusty said. "We stay sharp or we get sloppy, but we don't change."

"Quit connin' me," Saul said.

They watched the race. Rusty saw his opening.

"That your hound way in the back there?" Rusty said.

"He breaks late," Saul said. "Everyone knows this."

On the track, the dogs were coming around the back stretch, and the crowd on the bleachers rose, cheering. Number four started down the stretch run, passed one dog, then a second, a third. . . .

"You gonna treat me like a grown-up at least," Saul said, coming to his feet with the rest of the crowd, "tell me what the scam is?"

Under the noise, Rusty leaned over and whispered in Saul's ear.

Saul's eyes widened, then glazed over as all around him people were standing and shouting. Coming down the stretch, number four ran out of juice and fell back. Saul sat down even before the cheering crescendoed, announcing the finish. For his dog, the race was already over.

Rusty placed an envelope in Saul's lap, then got up and walked out as, on the track, number four crossed the finish line last by several lengths.

Saul considered his options. In one hand, a bunch of losing tickets. In the other, courtesy of Rusty Ryan and Danny Ocean, a ticket to Las Vegas.

He ripped the wager slips in half and tossed them on the ground. He popped a wedge of orange in his mouth and chewed thoughtfully. Best to do what the doctor ordered.

EIGHT

Santa Monica

"And Saul makes ten," Danny said as they picked at a plate of oysters in a hole-in-the-wall bar called Jay's in Santa Monica. Danny and Rusty both looked weary from all the recruitment.

A TV over the end of the bar played a promo for an upcoming Tyson fight set for Vegas.

"Ten should do it, don't you think?" Danny said, positioning an oyster for a trip down his gullet.

Rusty shrugged. He was trying to spear a slippery oyster with a little seafood fork.

"You think we need one more?" Danny asked, slurping the morsel from the shell, dabbing his lips with a linen napkin.

Rusty shrugged, jabbing at his oyster.

"You think we need one more," Danny repeated.

Rusty shrugged. He put the little fork down, picked up his oyster by the shell, and inhaled the damn thing.

"Okay," Danny said. "We'll get one more."

Chicago

The El was actually still elevated in parts—the Loop, for instance, that circled the downtown mercantile and financial center and gave it its name. But most of the El was underground in ancient dank tunnels that heaving Lake Michigan had been trying to invade since the very beginning.

Native Chicagoans seemed to have a sixth sense—El-car balance—that kept them relatively stable as the trains torqued and shook and shuddered on the curves and degraded straightaways of the aging subway system.

One passenger in particular—in a swaying, rush hour–crowded car toward the rear of a north-bound train—kept his footing as though he was gyroscoped. He was a handsome, dark-eyed, rather preppy-appearing young man who, but for the frayed leather jacket, might have been mistaken for a Chicago law student.

Linus was his name. And pursuit of the law was not his game.

Two overgroomed stockbrokers in beautifully tailored suits stood with their backs to the young man, yammering about high-interest yields, bumping lightly against each other and their fel-

low communters. Consequently, they didn't notice that Linus was slowly picking one of their
pockets.

Very slowly. The thievery was glacier-paced.

His face always forward and inscrutable,
Linus gingerly raised one tail of his target's
Brooks Brothers jacket. *Nice goods*, he thought as
he fingered the finely woven material. With in-
comparable dexterity, he unbuttoned the wallet
pocket of the man's suit pants with a flick of his
thumb and his forefinger.

From elsewhere in the train car, nothing appeared amiss, and no passenger looked the
wiser. Or so it seemed. . . .

Nearby, however, a copy of the *Chicago Sun-
Times*, half opened and held up in commuter-
reading position, came down just enough to
allow a pair of eyes to peer over it.

The eyes were locked on Linus.

Danny, a faint smirk on his lips, was casing
him. Danny was quite aware of the heist in
progress. So far, so good for Linus the preppy
heistmeister.

The young lifter had his spoils in sight—a
Gucci wallet. He waited for just the right moment, and when the train hit another curve, he
stumbled forward, his left hand finding support
on the stockbroker's shoulder.

"Sorry 'bout that," Linus said as his right hand
relieved the man of his wallet.

"No problem, guy," the banker said.

The stockbroker resumed his yacking, oblivious, as Linus tucked his prize into his own jacket pocket, his face betraying nothing.

Only Danny appreciated the artistry performed there at that moment.

He smiled to himself: The kid passed the test. He folded the *Sun-Times* under his arm, turned his back to Linus, and shifted imperceptibly in his direction.

When Union Station came up a few minutes later and the train squealed to a stop, Linus jumped out, leaving his prey aboard, one wallet lighter.

Half a moment later, Danny stepped off too.

In the hurly-burly of evening rush hour in Union Station, commuters zigged and zagged, crossing this way and that, all on furious schedules. Linus slipped blithely through them, in no hurry, a man who'd pulled this job a thousand times before.

He dodged and sidestepped the crazed nine-to-fivers, and except for a brief brush with one well-dressed man who had the *Sun-Times* tucked under his arm, he escaped the station without incident.

He walked a block or two up Michigan Avenue to make sure he had no tail—an old habit—and turned a corner onto a side street before casually reaching into his jacket to count his winnings

His face fell.

All he found where the stolen Gucci wallet once resided was a calling card. On one side, in engraved printing, were two words: DANIEL OCEAN. On the flip side, in handwriting:

Nice pull. Murphy's Bar, Rush & Division.

Linus stared at the card for a long minute, turning it over, then over again.

Twenty minutes later he walked into Murphy's Bar.

He walked through the busy saloon front to back, casing the joint, until he saw the Gucci wallet on a tabletop. Beside it stood a half-drunk bottle of Guinness and a half-empty glass.

Sitting at the same small table was Danny Ocean. So he assumed.

"Hi, Linus," Danny said. "Sit down."

"Who are you?" Linus said.

"A friend of Bobby Caldwell's. Sit down," Danny said.

Linus balked, prideful. He looked at Danny cool and long. But sense found a way, and he sat.

"Bobby told me about you," Danny said, "said you were the best set of hands he ever saw. Didn't expect to find you working wallets on the subway."

"That wasn't work. That was practice," Linus said. He slouched in his chair, leaning back away from the table.

Danny reached into his jacket and set a plane ticket on the table. But he kept his hand over it. "You're either in or out right now."

"What is it?" Linus said, unbudging.

"A plane ticket," Danny said. "A job offer."

"You're pretty trusting pretty fast," Linus said.

"Bobby has every faith in you," Danny said.

"Fathers are like that," Linus said.

Danny did a double-take. Father. That was news.

"He didn't tell you?" Linus said.

Danny shook his head, looking at the kid anew.

"He doesn't like me trading on his name," Linus said.

"You do this job, he'll be trading on yours," Danny said.

Linus leaned forward, picked up Danny's bottle of Guiness, and took a slug. "What if I say no?" he said.

"We'll get someone else who won't be quite as good," Danny said. "You can go back to feeling up stockbrokers."

Linus put the Guiness bottle down and considered. He looked at the ticket under Danny's hand, then at the wallet. It was one or the other.

A waitress passed, and Danny signaled her for his bill. When his attention returned to Linus, the wallet remained, but the ticket beneath his hand was gone. Linus was reading it.

"That's the best lift I've seen you make yet," Danny said.

"Las Vegas, huh?" Linus said.

"America's playground," Danny said with a smile.

NINE

Las Vegas

As a variety of gentlemen flew into Vegas from a variety of directions, and their passenger jets circled the city and descended into McCarran International Airport, they all saw the same mirage in the desert. A strange, isolated artifact of the human imagination.

Looming out of an expanse of harsh wilderness where no city was called for—where no trade routes or rivers had ever crossed, where no mineral or hydrocarbon wealth had been discovered, where no water source sprang from the ground, or crops or cattle gathered to market—in a nowhere spot on a nowhere landscape, was a city made in the 1940s by a clique of men with some spare change. Mobsters as city planners.

They wanted a city for gambling and sin in an overwhelmingly puritan country. They picked a state that in the beginning was a mining colony populated almost solely by single men, where gambling had already been legal for three-quarters of a century. It was still a saloon society dominated by hustlers and cowboys who were blithely uninterested in moral reform.

The perfect spot.

They made a lights-flashing, skyline-pulsing neon fortress that left good taste behind but invited folks to spend like fools on all the most corrupting, forbidden, damnation-inducing fun things they could think of.

It was a work of genius.

Hard cash came flowing in from all over America.

Sixty years later, the neon fortress had grown ever gaudier, ever grander, closer to the heavens than the medieval cathedrals had ever reached. Ever more tribute was tossed onto the collection plates. The Church of the Wild Side, where pilgrims were drawn to worship as though in a religious trance.

Fun seekers poured in.

And so did their money.

From their taxis on the way in from the airport—along with the traditional banners advertising the whole spectrum of entertainment from Siegfried and Roy's disappearing white tiger and elephant act for families, to topless female magicians and floor shows for big boys and girls—the gathering crew saw one promo that loomed larger than all the rest: an enormous billboard touting, as the fight to end all fights, the upcoming heavyweight boxing match between Mike Tyson and Lennox Lewis.

Below the big billboard, a hollering hawker waved fliers for gentlemen's clubs—meaning strip joints with lap dancing—and entertainment bureaus—outcall nude dancing/massage/ hooker services.

These guys knew what the shorthand meant. None of that was their speed. There was a panoply of more refined services available inside the casinos if sex was the name of their game.

It wasn't.

Money was. Spondulicks. Filthy lucre. Cabbage. Jack. Scratch.

But the gigantic prizefight billboard rising above the airport highway—that was actually a jumbo moneygram waving to them from their future, had they but known it. As it was, it just struck them as Vegas's usual attempt to market every event to the public as singularly memorable, like none other before or since.

If things went according to Danny Ocean's plan, the billboard would be right.

The Reuben Tishkoff mansion was dressed up for the ball: floodlights illuminating the facade, base strobes outlining the lush, transplanted greenery from property line to property line, underwater lights in the pool sending forth a bluegreen glow like an emerald as big as the Ritz.

A balmy Las Vegas night: only eighty degrees at nine in the evening.

The bar was fully stocked. The buffet table was overflowing. The help had done their thing and been sent home.

Frank Catton was already there, mixing himself a drink.

Ding-dong.

Unaccustomed as he was to responding personally to the doorbell chimes, Tishkoff heaved himself up from a lounge chair and shuffled toward the front. He opened his door to find a street gang.

"Trick or treat," Livingston said.

Livingston, Basher, Yen, the Malloys, Saul, and Linus crowded his doormat. A taxi van pulled away behind them.

"What?" Tishkoff said. "You guys get a group rate?"

It was a munificent setting and a magnificent party. Wine and booze loosened lips and stories of great hilarity were told of heroic feats by men absent and present. And all of the stories were absolutely true, except the ones that were lies.

At the buffet table along one wall of Tishkoff's living room, Virgil and Turk piled shrimp onto plates as Saul pocketed a couple of oranges for later.

"You make it out to Utah much, Saul?" Turk said. Turk and his brother were Mormons, peace loving good boys.

"Not as much as I'd like," said Saul, the last man you'd ever see in the Mormon Tabernacle Choir.

"You should," Turk said. "You'd like it. You'd like Provo."

"Anybody see the salsa goes with this?" Virgil said, scarfing down a jumbo shrimp. He was the shyer brother; he left the social small talk to Turk.

At the wet bar, Basher mixed a drink called a Cabo Eel for Livingston. On a couch, Yen balanced coffee table ornaments into a skyscraper to Frank's astonishment.

In a corner, off on his own, Linus watched the company, his eyes narrowing, wary. He was not privy to the social ways of these old warhorses. His father, an associate of theirs on various enterprises over the years, had kept a firewall between his work and his home for most of Linus's youth. Linus had not yet found a comfort zone in this Vegas palazzo.

If he were going to, it would be soon or never.

"Gentlemen," Danny announced, "welcome to Las Vegas."

Danny stood at the top of the low, carpeted stairs leading into the room, flanked by Rusty and Tishkoff. He stared down. "Everybody eaten?" he said.

Grunts and gratified murmurs.

"Good," he said. "Everybody sober?"

A few laughs.

"Close enough," he went on. "Most of you know each other already. You probably haven't met Linus Caldwell before—he's Bobby's kid outta Chicago."

Linus traded nods around the room.

"Okay," Danny said. "Before we start, nobody's on the line here yet. What I'm about to propose to you happens to be both highly lucrative and highly dangerous." He looked from face to face to let that reality gel a little. "If that doesn't sound like your particular brand of vodka, help yourself to as much food as you like and safe journey. No hard feelings."

He paused soberly. Then, turning away, he said, "Otherwise, come with me." He walked out of the living room, crossed the hall and entered another big room, the game room.

Rusty started to follow behind him, turning back briefly to cast an eye over the carefully chosen and assembled operatives, who at that moment looked like a bunch of openmouthed mooks.

It was crunch time.

Rusty continued into the next room.

The guys closed their mouths and looked each other over, sizing things up.

"What the hell?" Basher said. And he followed.

Almost immediately, so did Frank and Livingston.

Then Virgil, Turk, and Yen. Yen took the four-step landing with a single smooth bounce.

Saul took a last drink of iced tea, shook his head at his own incorrigible stupidity, and started up the stairs. He paused as he got a little shot of ulcer pain. And went on.

That left Linus, watching the line of men disappear. He was still on the fence. What did he know from Danny Ocean?

He turned to find Tishkoff by his side, staring at him. "Hi," Linus said.

"You're Bobby Caldwell's kid, huh?" Tishkoff said.

"Yeah," Linus said. *A little scary, this Tishkoff guy*, he thought.

"From Chicago?" Tishkoff asked.

"Yeah," Linus said.

"It's nice there," Tishkoff said. "You like it?"

"Yeah," Linus said. *Maybe he's not so bad.* He started to relax.

"That's wonderful," Tishkoff said. "Get in the goddamn room."

TEN

The richly appointed game room showcased a tournament-size, tournament-quality pool table at center stage. It had a panel of three large TV monitors on one side wall, a maxisize rear-projection TV at one end, a full bar, two electronic pinball machines, an old-fashioned Brit-style darts setup, and a miniature video arcade in one corner.

But the men noticed nothing else besides what was on the pool table.

Atop its green felt sat a raised, elaborate miniature of Terry Benedict's Las Vegas: three casinos and resort hotels with the Strip running between them.

As the eleven men surrounded the table and the model, their concerns faded away. Their fascination with the superbly executed and detailed model took over.

"Gentlemen, the 14,000 block of Las Vegas Boulevard," Danny said. "Otherwise known as the Bellagio, the Mirage, the MGM Grand. Together, they're three of the most profitable casinos in Las Vegas."

Danny removed the Strip from the model. The men crowded close to look. Revealed beneath was a complex substructure that united the three casinos underground. There were three tunnels, one leading from each casino and joining at a single, freight-size elevator shaft, which in turn descended into an enormous vault.

"Gentlemen, the Bellagio vault," Danny said. "Located below the Strip, beneath two hundred feet of solid earth. It safeguards every dime that comes through each of the three casinos above it."

A moment of appreciative silence as the men took in the tidy logic of the plan.

"And we're going to rob it," Danny said.

Everyone murmured a kind of awed reverence of the notion, thinking no farther than the nifty model before them

"Smash-and-grab job, huh?" Linus said.

"It's a little more complicated than that," Rusty said.

Danny picked up a remote control and flipped on the panel of TVs.

"Courtesy of Frank Catton, new blackjack dealer at the Bellagio," said Danny, "security tapes from the three casinos."

He keyed the remote.

On the monitors, three separate montages played—black-and-white security tapes. Each tape followed the journey a cash load would take, starting at the fortified cashier cages in each casino, moving into and down the tunnels, then uniting underground at the elevator shaft. There, with the same image now showing on all three TVs, the cash pallet pushed into the elevator, descended, and finally exited into the large vault.

The group's glances shot back and forth from the TV to the corresponding section of the model, from the point of view inside the tunnel to the miniature tunnel itself.

"Okay," Danny said. "Bad news first."

The ten other men looked up from the model to the master of ceremonies. How bad could it be, given the expertise demonstrated so far?

"This place," Danny said, "houses a security system which rivals nuclear missile silos. First, we have to get within the casino cages."

"Here, here, and here," Rusty said, indicating the positions on the model.

"Which anyone knows takes more than a smile," Danny said.

"Next, we have to get through these doors to the tunnels, each of which requires a different six-digit code changed every twelve hours."

Danny paused to let the men digest that information.

"Past those lies the elevator," he said, "and this is where it gets tricky. The elevator won't move without authorized fingerprint identification."

"Which we can't fake," Rusty added.

"And vocal confirmations from both the security center within the Bellagio and the vault below," Danny said.

"Which we won't get," Rusty finished.

"Furthermore," Danny said, "the elevator shaft is rigged with motion detectors."

"Meaning if we manually override the lift," Rusty said, "the shaft's exit will lock down automatically and we'll be trapped."

He looked around to see how the men were taking the bad news.

So far so good. No outright looks of horror.

"Once we've gotten down the shaft, though," Danny said, "it's a walk in the park. Just three more guards with Uzis and predilections toward not being robbed, and the most elaborate vault door conceived by man. Any questions?"

Silence. For a moment, each man kept his two dozen questions—or objections—to himself. A discouraging picture really. At last, someone spoke up.

The Amazing Yen rattled off something in Cantonese, gesturing and pointing at the model. Of course, no one understood him. Except Rusty.

"No," Rusty said in response. "Tunneling is out. There are Richter sensors monitoring the ground for one hundred yards in every direction. If a groundhog tried to nest there, they'd know about it. Anyone else?"

Another silence. Either the guys were too

dumbfounded by that bilingual exchange or too benumbed by the task ahead of them to speak.

"You said something about good news," Turk said.

Danny smiled, happy someone asked about the good-news part of the equation.

"The Nevada Gaming Commission stipulates a casino must hold in reserve enough cash to cover every chip at play on its floor," he said, walking around the group, moving from face to face as he talked like a college professor doling out his pearls of wisdom.

"As I mentioned," he went on, "this vault services each of the three casinos above it. That means during the week, by law, it must hold anywhere from sixty to seventy million dollars in cash and coin."

A meaningful silence ensued.

"On a weekend, between eighty and ninety million."

Even more potent silence.

"On a fight night, like the one two weeks from tonight, the night we're going to rob it, at least a hundred and fifty million. Without breaking a sweat."

He stopped in his original spot before the monitors and gazed around the room. "Now there are eleven of us," he said. "Each with an equal share. You do the math."

As he scanned their ten faces around the table, he saw everyone doing precisely that in their

heads. Except Virgil, who did it on his fingers—
and then whistled.

"That's what I said," Rusty said.

Everyone seemed suitably impressed by his
share.

Danny, Rusty, and Tishkoff had had plenty of
time to compute a share exactly. Everyone else,
except Saul, just made a rough estimate. They
knew it would be somewhere between ten million and fifteen million each. Close enough when
the numbers were that big.

Saul, naturally, had the exact number in his
head almost as soon as the proposition was on
the table: $13,636,363.63 each.

"I have a question," he said to Danny.

Danny turned toward him.

"Say we do get into the cage," Saul said in his
grumbly voice, "and through the security doors
there, and down the elevator we can't move, and
past the guards with guns, and into the vault we
can't open—"

"Without being seen by the cameras," Rusty
said.

"Oh, right," Danny said, responding to everyone's renewed alarm. "I forgot to mention the
cameras."

"Say we do all that," said Saul. "We're just
supposed to walk outta there with a hundred
and fifty million dollars in cash on us without
getting stopped?"

Danny smiled his broad, sure-of-himself grin.
"Yeah."

Like that, Saul's ulcer flared up, and he popped a Rolaid into his mouth. He looked panic-stricken: His $13,636,363.63 retirement kitty, so thrilling to hold in his mind a moment ago, was going up in smoke as he stood there. This guy Danny Ocean—he was as mad as a moonbeam.

"All right," Danny said, with that same knowing smile. "Here's how we'll begin . . ."

ELEVEN

"First task: reconnaissance," Danny said, looking first at Linus. "I want to know everything that's going on in all three casinos. From the rotation of the dealers to the path of every cash cart."

Two weeks they had to prepare. It seemed like plenty of time.

Linus, with his ability to look one way and watch another, went to get the lowdown on operations at the MGM Grand Hotel Casino.

It was the biggest of the big—112 acres, 5009 rooms. It had four thirty-story towers, an emerald-green exterior, and a big roaring bronze lion out front, in keeping with the Emerald City/Hollywood theme of the decor.

Linus simply walked in through the front door—it used to be a gargantuan lion's mouth with ferocious teeth, but kids were scared to enter, and families turned around and went to

other hotels. A more conventionally grand portal
now welcomed Linus's arrival.

He passed the statue of Dorothy from *The Wizard of Oz* in the front rotunda and was presented
with the choice of thirty-three acres of rides,
shows, street performers, restaurants, and other
diversions.

Not his cup of green tea. He headed for the
gambling floor, just another young customer
with years of profligacy ahead of him, which
was how a floor manager or pit boss would view
him if they saw him saunter in. Fresh meat. Treat
him nice.

Linus wandered through the gaming floor,
checking out the hardware: the location of the
eyes in the sky hidden in light fixtures, the expanses of large two-way mirrors, the inconspicuous security doors behind pillars and planters
from which muscle would emerge as needed.

Linus and the rest of the eleven were keenly
aware that the aura of openness and license at
the casinos, the let-your-hair-down, anything-goes atmosphere of the place, was a carefully
nurtured illusion. A join-the-party, round-the-clock bacchanal was the sell; keep the games
rolling smoothly and get the rubes' money was
the actuality.

A Vegas gambling casino was one of the most
rigidly controlled places on earth. Just beneath
the surface, it was a tightly monitored, strictly
disciplined, authoritarian organization. Just behind the curtain, a Praetorian guard of private

thugs waited on a hair trigger to spring out and brutally terminate any hoopla that threatened to get out of hand and disrupt play.

Linus made himself invisible sitting at a blackjack table, immersed in the flow of the cards, losing small amounts of money. Only with the eyes in the back of his head did he notice the cash cart emerging from the casino innards, pushed by security guards past tourists, cocktail waitresses, and low rollers sitting at the blackjack table, on a set route each time.

Two weeks until the takedown seemed like a lot of time. But there was a lot they needed to know.

"I wanna know everything about every guard," Danny said to Frank. "Every watcher, anyone with a security pass. I wanna know where they're from, what their nicknames are, how they take their coffee."

Frank was a pro. He'd been on the Bellagio payroll—as a new blackjack dealer—for less than a week, and already he'd been able to supply the team with security tapes from all three Terry Benedict casinos.

The Bellagio was the newest of the Benedict casinos—just three years old—and the poshest. A towering, arc-shaped structure, it looked down on a twelve-acre man-made grotto and a faux Italian village. Immense dancing fountains shot skyward from the lake twenty-four hours a day, illuminated by multicolored spotlights. The height of luxury was what Terry Benedict craved in building the Bellagio, in pursuit of which he laid in romantic botanical gardens, chichi European furniture and a fortune in fine art. The Bellagio was his masterpiece. He was in love with the place.

And Frank Catton was in love with the idea of stealing Benedict's darling blind. He went in under her skirts, as it were—spending a lot of quality time in the employees' break room. He hung out there, sucking up technical info as well as a flood of human-factors material.

Two security technicians on a smoke break nattered about their sex lives. They chattered about their work schedules, who had the better shifts, where they went to coop—sneak a nap— after they'd lucked out with an all-nighter with a willing Keno girl or a weekend warrior, a secretary in from Phoenix or LA, in town for a sex blowout. One of them had found a steamy new strip club in downtown Vegas where the girls were "cherce."

Across the room, Frank sat innocently doing a crossword. Well, it looked as though he were doing a crossword. In fact he was casually jotting an exact transcript of the technicians' conversation.

And he was noting down the names, job classification, and color coding on the electronic keycards clipped to the techies' belts.

* * *

"Most of all," Danny said as he gave the Malloy brothers their marching orders, "I want you guys to know these casinos. They were built as labyrinths to keep people in. I want you guys to know the quick routes out."

Indeed, the casinos were built to keep people there in every way possible. They were conceived psychologically as hermetically sealed fantasy worlds—no windows to the outside revealing the time of day, no clocks, the same festive lighting and neutral internal climate twenty-four by seven, no reminders that a real world of duty and drudgery existed beyond the seductive cocoon.

Eat there, drink there, sleep right there in the casino hotel—that was the prescription for patrons. Don't go far from the gambling tables.

Sex?

For high rollers, don't even think of driving out of Las Vegas's Clark County to any of the thirty legal brothels in Nye county or elsewhere in Nevada. That would be three or four potential gambling hours lost. At some establishments, a casino girl or house girl would appear magically by the side of a high roller as soon as the casino host perceived he might be getting bored and needed an hour's diversion before getting back to the tables. For the not-so-high rollers, a sexual encounter that would walk right up and knock on the door to his hotel room was only a phone call away, thanks to the technically illegal but silently condoned and ubiquitously advertised entertainment bureaus.

Turk and Virgil Malloy clomped into the Mirage and gawked like schoolboys. Apart from the fifty-foot-high erupting volvano outside, the place had animals! It was a tropical palace with its own indoor rain forest. It had a white-tiger habitat, a shark aquarium, a dolphin house, and a secret garden. The Malloy boys were in heaven. Only a cell-phone call from Rusty got them back to work.

With pockets full of quarters they lumbered in to play the slots and found that many of the slots were now completely electronic. Slip in your credit card or bank debit card and play; pour your hard-earned money down the rat hole the easy way. The Malloys stuck with the blue-haired ladies playing the hard-currency coin slots. Feet-on-the-ground kind of boys, they needed to feel the physical weight of their losses—and occasional gains—as they experienced them.

The whole time they were at the slots or the roulette wheel or the Keno lounge, of course, they were working.

They picked out one front-entrance guard and shadowed him on his shift change. They watched him approach an employees-only area and swipe a keycard through a keypad—a keycard identical to the one Frank was scoping out at the Bellagio. Lights on the keypad flashed red to green, admitting the guard into the employees-only doorway.

The keycard system wasn't so bad—keycards could be lifted or duplicated. But there was also, standing by the door, a uniformed sentry. And there was also, above the door, a security camera embedded in the ceiling. No one walked through that portal unchecked and unapproved.

Their job done, the Malloys started toward the casino's exit in different directions. They began to argue. The shortest way out was this way. No, it was that way.

Two weeks they had to solve the casinos. Two weeks began to look like barely time enough to get started, for all the ins and outs the Danny Ocean Irregulars had to master.

"Second task: power," Danny had said. As Basher Tarr waited for the light to turn green on Las Vegas Boulevard outside the three casinos with dozens of other tourists, Danny's charge echoed in his head. "On the night of the fight, we're gonna throw the switch on Sin City. Basher, it's your show."

The Strip shimmered now in the scalding sun, teeming with families—hardly like the Sin City they all knew and loved. Instead it was Dad and Mom and biblical multitudes of kids. Overheated, whining, screaming, power-loading sugar drinks and carbo indigestibles.

Mom and Dad were not there, as of yore, for the big-ticket lounge acts and glamorous, bare-breasted floor shows. Dad and Mom were dragging their three-point-four kids down the boulevard, gaping at the gigantic pyramid that was really just a hotel, or the phony volcano that spewed fire and water "lava" every fifteen minutes, and the cascade of other amusement park/video arcade features that made up the "New Vegas."

This new family Las Vegas wasn't going to last.

So proclaimed the Eleven in a moment of boozy ebullience after one of their hardworking planning sessions. The real money in Vegas was in gambling—in the open-fisted, compulsive, hey-it's-only-once-a-year prodigality of the visitors who came for the thrill of Vegas-style gambling—gambling dressed up in sex. Blatant, frank, unapologetic, everywhere-you-looked sex.

Wave pools and roller coasters and tiger acts were fun, but not adult fun.

Sex would be back. Topless would be back. On that, they all agreed.

The lights would come up on a once-again X-rated Las Vegas before long.

But before they did, Basher's job was to try to douse the lights of the present city.

He crossed the street with the mass of folk, and when he saw a manhole cover, he stopped. Extracting a small metal hook from his jacket, he removed the manhole from its perch, so matter-of-fact, business-as-usual about the action that no passerby looked twice at him.

Basher dropped into the hole and pulled the heavy cover over him, and not a person within eyeshot gave him a second thought.

It took half the power output of the Hoover Dam on the Colorado to light up the Strip. So much energy pulsed into and through this gaudy casino village that astronauts regularly spotted it from the shuttle—and savored their distance from it.

Basher knew one small thing about the big river of electricity that kept Vegas lit around the clock. When it stepped down from the high-voltage, long-distance trunk lines into lower-voltage, locally useable power feeds, it did so at a relay station. And that relay station, where coils, capacitors, transformers, and switches hummed and sparked under their incessant load, was underground—under the Strip itself.

It was a small connecting point between the thundering high-dam source and a billion separate little glowing bulbs.

A choke point.

Basher's job was to design a noose to choke it down to nothing.

"Third task: surveillance," Danny had said at the planning session. "Casino security has an eye and an ear on everything, so we'll want an eye and ear on them, Livingston."

The Bellagio was the Terry Benedict operations headquarters and the nerve center of the

three target casinos. Dell Livingston, the nervous, touchy surveillance tech, would have to
bring his genius to bear there. He would have to
penetrate the Bellagio's hard drive, as it were,
and work his way out to the peripherals.

The Bellagio Security Center, located one floor
above the gambling floor, was unimaginatively
called the "Eye in the Sky" by the casino's operators. It was an impressively large, up-to-date,
electronic-surveillance facility, designed to observe everything that moved anywhere near the
gambling and money operations.

Hundreds of monitors manned by dozens of
watchers canvassed the fan of gambling tables
on the floor below.

In a separate alcove of the center was another
bank of monitors manned by two watchers,
whom the team dubbed Fat and Slim. These two
oversaw a different section of the casino: the
cage where the cashiers sat and converted
money and chips back and forth, as well as the
underground tunnels and the elevator that led to
the vault. Everything, in fact, that the team had
seen in miniature in Tishkoff's game room.

Only NASA's control rooms at the Johnson
Space Center in Houston housed more technology than the security center, but not by much.

Dell Livingston's eighth-floor room at the Bellagio was a counter nerve center to the hotel's. It
was a virus hungry to invade.

A set of schematics of the Bellagio was spread
out on a table—a page of the set Danny and

Rusty had "borrowed" from J. A. Kuehn & Associates, Architects. Danny and Livingston bent over it, studying its details.

"Well," Livingston said, "it's not the least accessible system I've seen, but it's close. I don't suppose they have a closed-circuit feed I could tap into."

Danny shook his head. No such luck.

"Then this is definitely a black-bag job," Livingston said. "Do they employ an in-house technician?"

Danny looked to Rusty who, behind them, was tinkering with Livingston's audiovideo setup: several portable monitors, a laptop and modem, telephone headsets, and other arrays. Livingston jumped to stop Rusty before he hit the wrong buttons.

"Two," Rusty said, "and one of them is lonely."

TWELVE

The Olympic Gardens Strip Club, in a slightly seedy part of downtown Las Vegas far away from the resort casinos on the Strip, ironically represented the erotic future of the Strip itself—if Danny Oceans's eleven-man think tank was to be believed.

It was a "gentleman's club"—a hard-core strip bar where, after their runway dances, the strippers descended into the audience and recruited clients for visits to individual booths for private dances. The raunchiness and the contact intensity of the lap dances depended on how much the girl was willing to do for the amount of money offered. It was an odd hybrid transaction, with the girl nude but the guy dressed, and stopping short of any contact of naked parts. No actual sex acts took place. Much close-up display and seminaked rubbing occured. For about three minutes. And a small fee.

Safe sex?

Safe something.

More like near sex for guys on low budgets.

One lap dance at the Olympic Gardens on the third night of the Eleven's prep campaign featured a lovely, long-limbed, auburn-haired maiden with a smile that could melt methane ice. Her client was one of the lonely security technician Frank Catton had eavesdropped upon at the Bellagio.

So warm and congenial was the young woman, and so smitten with the close-up view of her bare, perfect breasts was the not-exactly-sober tech, that he had already shelled out three twenties to keep the encounter going. As she ground her comely pelvis against his chest, and he pawed at her midriff, the dancer discreetly removed the electronic keycard from his belt. And abruptly, although the song—and the time—wasn't over, she dismounted and gave his cheek a caress. "I'll be right back, honey," she said. "Don't move a muscle."

"Depends on the muscle," the tech slurred, wasted and in love.

She pouted, flirtingly, as she did for every idiot who dropped a line like that, then made her way between tables and quickly down the hall and outside the club.

Rusty, waiting for her against his car, smiled as she emerged, clad only in a silk throw. "Thanks, Charmaine," he said as she slipped him the keycard.

He slipped her some c-notes in return. "I'll

have it back within the hour. Say hello to your mom for me."

"Say it yourself," the dancer said. "She'll be onstage in five minutes." She dashed back inside. A lucrative night, and it wasn't over yet.

A bunch of fat, primary-colored helium balloons floated just above the crowd, making their way across the Bellagio Casino, all wishing somebody happy anniversary!

As the delivery boy who carried the ballons passed an employees-only door, complete with its own sentry and embedded ceiling camera, he bumped into a tourist—and the balloons drifted out of his hands and up into the camera's lens.

Virgil Malloy adjusted his delivery cap, and as he turned to grab the balloons' strings, he bumped into a tourist.

"Hey, watch it, bud."

Surprise, surprise. The tourist was Turk Malloy.

Inside, in the Bellagio's "Eye in the Sky," the watcher known as Slim suddenly went blind on his far right monitor. Festive, brightly colored balloons filled the entire frame. Slim was on the case in an instant. He keyed his walkie-talkie. "433, we have visual impairment on the east door camera 433."

Sentry 433, standing at a watchful distance by the cage door, snapped out of his reverie watching the spinning roulette wheel. "Check," he barked low into his walkie-talkie and strode toward the balloons hovering in front of the embedded camera.

"Excuse me, sir," he said as he approached the delivery boy. "You're going to have to move your balloons." He pointed.

Virgil was too busy picking a fight with Turk to listen.

"Who you calling bud, pal?" Virgil said.

"Who you calling *pal*, friend?" Turk said.

"Who you calling friend," Virgil said, flailing for another epithet. Failing one, he said, "Bud."

With the sentry out of position and preoccupied with the two doofuses, a newly arrived man dressed in a technician's uniform moved quickly to the door and swiped his newly acquired keycard.

Livingston.

When the keypad flashed red to green, he entered.

He found himself in the hallway adjacent to the money cage. He was in—past the first line of defense. In the lion's cage. And suddenly perspiring freely. This was not a man whose nervous system fit him well for black ops. And yet he pressed on, sheer guts apparently not his problem. He took a moment to wipe his brow and check his palm: drawn there, in ballpoint, was a diagram of the cage corridors.

In the "Eye in the Sky," on a monitor adjacent to the balloon-clouded one, Livingston appeared. And nonchalantly, as if he belonged there, he ambled down a hallway, then another, until he approached the security center itself.

He paused by an unmarked door beside the entrance door to the security center.

He swiped his keycard to enter. A lock clicked open.

He found himself, as planned, in the circuitry room. It was a giant walk-in closet with a switchboard full of wires, plugs, lights, fuses, switches, shunts, and other electronic control gear.

Another power transfer choke point.

Livingston went to work. In a flurry, as if he were diffusing a bomb, he spliced into the tangle of wires and cables, never taking a second look. He was in his element.

"You heard about this new medical discovery they made?" Virgil said, still nose to nose with Turk by the employees-only door—still accidentally blocking the sentry from the balloons. "It's called a sense of direction. Apparently we're all supposed to have one."

"Yeah, yeah, yeah, whatever, balloon boy," Turk said, doing his best to make the epithet sound nasty and demeaning.

"Gentlemen, gentlemen," the sentry said.

Livingston's work in the circuitry room was going swiftly, but still wasn't quite done. There remained one thing to do. He clipped a small mechanism known as a spider—it was tiny, black, antennaless, and easily hidden in dark places—to a main conduit. He checked a tiny receiver he held in his hand. Bingo! It was picking up the spider's sound web.

One last click into place . . .

Simultaneously, inside the "Eye in the Sky," a brief blip wiggled across Slim's monitors. Slim, agitated by the damn balloons, failed to notice.

Simultaneously, upstairs in the Bellagio Hotel in Dell Livingston's suite, a bank of TV monitors came alive, feeding all the same views that Fat and Slim saw on their monitors downstairs: the cage and its doors, its tunnels, the elevator, the vault.

Danny and Rusty smiled widely at the sudden and welcome transmission. A big hurdle, overcome.

"Why do they paint hallways that color?" Danny said.

"They say taupe is very soothing," Rusty said.

His job done, Livingston exhaled and stepped out of the circuitry room. He moved down the hallway the way he had come, wiping the sweat from his brow with his palm. He came to an intersection, looked left, looked right, checked his palm for the corridor directions.

His sweat had smeared the little map on his palm. Indecipherable.

He was flying blind.

He looked both ways again, trying to remember which way he came in.

Having no idea.

* * *

Up in the suite, Danny and Rusty watched as Livingston hesitated, then started down the corridor to his left.

"Uh-oh," Danny said. Dead ahead of Livingston was Fat, moving purposefully his way. Danny and Rusty held their breath. This could be the whole enchilada right here.

Livingston and Fat drew nearer . . . and passed each other.

"Hiya," Fat said to the unfamiliar-looking security tech.

"Fine, thanks," Livingston answered and continued on, thinking he was in the clear. Especially when he saw the exit looming ahead.

Danny and Rusty let out their breath.

But then Fat turned behind him and hailed him back. "Hey," Fat said.

Just on the other side of the employees-only cage door, sentry 433 had at last outmaneuvered Virgil and Turk, and grabbed the balloons himself.

Virgil quickly snatched them back. "Hey! Get your own balloons," he said. He finally moved on, continuing on his way down the edge of the gaming floor, then crossing toward the bar.

Turk threw him a finger and ambled off in the other direction.

433 shook his head. Every day it was something completely different.

* * *

On the other side of the door—panicking, ignoring Fat's summons—Livingston approached the exit's keypad and swiped his keycard, desperate to slip out and melt away. But the keypad light remained red.

"Hey," Fat said, on his tail.

Livingston looked; he'd swiped the wrong side of his keycard. He tried again. It flashed to green.

He pulled the door toward him.

Fat moved up on him and blocked it.

Upstairs, Danny and Rusty leaned forward and stared at the screen, certain that Livingston had had it.

To have done this much and come this far. To have it end just as they were hitting their stride . . .

It wasn't right. Lady Luck had left them high and dry.

In the half-open exit below, Fat said to Livingston, "Hey, you dropped this." He held out Livingston's receiver and placed it in his hand.

"Thanks," Livingston said, nodding at the big guard.

And he was out.

THIRTEEN

How did they spell relief in Livingston's suite upstairs at the Bellagio? It came from both guys' mouths in a rush, and was unprintable. And it ended in elated whoops and high-fives.

"Well," Danny said, calming just a little.

"Yeah," Rusty said as he leaned against a chair.

Then, just as quickly, they put the close call behind them. An inch was as good as a mile in their business. They were in.

"Fourth task: construction," Danny said.

The warehouse in a light-industrial quarter out toward the airport was a property Reuben Tishkoff had picked up a few years back as partial payment on a gambling debt of a local one-time high roller. He had used it to store extra furniture and equipment from his hotel. Now half empty, it was just a sore reminder of his lost pleasure palace.

How sweet it was for him to use it to construct Terry Benedict's comeuppance.

The gang hauled in building materials: lumber, tools, paint, facing materials. And the architectural drawings. Yen was an invaluable time saver, hauling three times his share, carrying objects on his head, shoulders, and arms, a circus act with a hardware store.

"We need to build an exact working replica of the Bellagio vault," Danny said by way of directions. He set up a VCR and monitor so they could work off the actual security tapes.

"We'll need it for practice," Rusty said.

"Something like that," Danny said. He'd explain more on a need-to-know schedule. No point giving the men more to get nervous about than they already had.

As Linus hauled in materials, Danny took him aside. "Our fifth task is intelligence," he said to the young hand. "We need those codes, Linus. From the only man who has all three."

"Benedict," Linus said. Linus was cool. He was learning how to think a step ahead.

"Learn to love his shadow," Danny said. He gave the kid no more direction than that. Linus had shown he was a professional. Best to let his instincts develop an approach that suited his talents.

"Wait, wait, wait," Linus said. "All I get to do is *watch* him?"

Danny looked him in the eyes. "For now. You gotta walk before you crawl."

Off of Linus' confused look, Rusty leaned in and said to the eager young pickpocket, "Reverse that."

Danny walked toward the Malloys. "Sixth task," he said to the brothers, throwing his arms around their shoulders. "Transport."

Downtown Las Vegas is as nondescript as any other parched, hardscrabble, midsize Western city—except for the slot machines in every other gas station and convenience store and the tacky minicasinos dotted all over town.

Car dealerships in Vegas are as gaudy and depressing as anywhere, the same faux-festive flags and decor, the same would-be-slick sales types with the same selling scams. "I might be able to slip you in under a fleet discount deal I just closed with one of the big hotels—but you'd have to jump on it right now today."

Billy Tim's van and truck dealership did not enjoy the best commercial address in town. It was on the outskirts, on a state highway leading into the mountains. It did not look prosperous. There were not a lot of shoppers on the dusty lot.

That was exactly why Frank picked Billy Tim's—Billy Tim himself would probably be hungry to make any deal that came his way.

Out on the lot, Turk and Virgil did the actual shopping: they seesawed up and down on opposite bumpers of a van, testing its shocks.

Inside, Frank negotiated with Billy Tim, a Cal Worthington–wannabe redneck huckster with a genuine drawl. Billy Tim was only half paying attention to Frank, fretting over what the Malloys were doing to his bouncing vehicles outside.

"I'm real sorry," Billy Tim said. "Eighteen-five each is the best offer I can make you."

"Oh, I understand perfectly," Frank said, enunciating his words ever so clearly—playing a bit of a dandy for Billy Tim's sake. "They are beautiful vans. Well, I thank you for your time . . ."

"Denham. Billy Tim Denham," Billy Tim said.

"Yes, Denham, like jeans," Frank said. They shook. And as they did, Frank looked down at Billy Tim's hands with sudden interest.

"You know, you have lovely hands," Frank said. "Do you moisturize?"

"I'm sorry?" Billy Tim said.

Frank didn't let go of the man's hand, holding on to it appreciatively.

"I swear by it," Frank said. "I try all sorts of lotions. I went through a fragrance-free period last year, but now I'm liking this new brand fortified with rose hip. My sister, you know—she uses the aloe vera with the sunscreen built in."

Billy Tim's face was rearranging itself into a sick, uncomfortable expression. Perfect. The object now being to force Billy Tim into lowering his price just to get Frank out of his office.

Billy Tim just couldn't get his hand back. "Uh-huh," Billy Tim said. "You said you'd be willing to pay in cash?"

"I did," Frank said. "You know, they say cinnamon is wonderful for your pores. Read that on the Internet. And that ideally you should be wearing gloves to bed, but I find that would interfere with my social agenda. Problem is, I get a reaction to camphor so I can't use traditional remedies—"

"If you could pay cash," Billy Tim said, "I could probably drop the price a little. To, say, seventeen—"

Frank squeezed his delicious hand a little more.

"Sixteen each!" Billy Tim said.

"That would be lovely," Frank said with a big coy smile.

FOURTEEN

In the Tishkoff warehouse, with the construction going apace and the clone of the Bellagio vault rising before their eyes, Danny stepped back to think.

The director for a show like this had to keep all the balls in the air and all the ponies prancing at once, but to different tunes. Timing was all-important. Like a chef, Danny had to have all the dishes prepped and in the oven in the right order, ready to serve at just the right time.

Reviewing his list of tasks on his fingers, Danny sensed he was missing something. "Power, surveillance, transport," he counted, half out loud.

"Anything I can do?" Tishkoff said.

Danny's eyes flashed from Tishkoff to Saul behind him. Saul, dressed in his usual frumpy attire, flashed a light on the dark spot—that was what Danny had missed.

"Get your wallet," Danny said to Tishkoff.

*   *   *

The hotels on the Strip had built-in shopping promenades—malls with a good dose of top-end shops. Fine men's clothiers. Haberdashers. Imported tailors. Hugely expensive places.

And they did good business. People came to Vegas with money, expecting to leave it there. They came with the notion that whatever they came with was already spent. So enjoy.

If they happened to win, they felt expansive. They liked to blow a little of it. How fortunate the good shops were there to serve them the very best.

A tailor in one of the finest shops fitted Saul for a half dozen suits—the finest labels Reuben Tishkoff's money could buy.

Saul smoothed out a coat sleeve. "This is nice material," he said.

"It's Armani, Saul," Danny said impatiently.

"It's very nice," Saul said.

Saul wasn't fooling anyone. He was scared, right down to his Florsheims.

Danny nodded to the tailor. The tailor stepped out of the fitting room.

"Saul, you're sure you're ready to do this?" Danny said.

Saul turned away, and when he faced Danny again, his entire aspect had changed: his features stone, his eyes icicles. "If you ever question me again, Daniel," he said, "you won't wake up the following morning."

They exchanged a long, fierce glance; Saul's eyes never wavered.

"You're ready," Danny said.

Danny signaled Tishkoff. They walked out of the fitting room together.

Saul immediately slumped into his old self. Looking to the set of mirrors, he practiced. "Hello," he said. "My name is Lyman Zerga."

Next time a little deeper: "My name is Lyman Zerga."

He continued practicing in front of Danny and Tishkoff in the limo as they made their way down the Strip. He wasn't shy about it. He was more than a con. More like a professional actor who loved the challenge of the role rather than the score.

Danny and Tishkoff knew the drill. They observed with critical approval as Saul worked his way into his character by talking incessantly to himself, trying out different voices and tones.

Saul was dressed completely and immaculately in fine Worsted, with his hair slicked back, a brief mustache on his lip, and impenetrably dark glasses riding the bridge of his nose. He continued to practice, his accent even deeper now, obscuring any specific geographic origin. Trans-European. He could be Scottish or Israeli.

"My name is Lyman Zerga. My name is Lyman Zerga," Saul said. If you couldn't do it so it came off naturally in front of friends, you would surely blow it when you had to take the stage for real.

Danny passed him an envelope packed with hundred-dollar bills.

"There's a little over twenty grand in there, Saul," Danny said. "Try to make it last."

Saul patted down his pockets for something he couldn't find. "You seen my—"

"Bought you a fresh roll," Danny said, handing him his antacids.

The limo pulled in the entrance drive to the Bellagio. It eased over to the curb short of the valet stand and pulled to a stop.

On the sidewalk outside, there was a flurry of footsteps approaching, and Saul's door swung open. Turk and Virgil stood waiting for him, both costumed as bodyguards: black blazers, dark glasses, walkie-talkie earpieces, blunt-toed black brogans, mean looks.

"Mr. Zerga, we're here," Virgil said.

"Good luck, Lyman," Danny said.

"Luck is for losers," Saul said, hesitating for just a second as he gathered himself. Then he climbed out onto the pavement, straightened up, and vanished. In his place was Lyman Zerga, a visiting powerhouse looking up critically at the facade of this would-be stylish fantasy hotel. He adjusted his dark glasses, checked his attaché case, and strode toward the entrance.

Inside, a steady stream of guests and casino patrons crisscrossed the Bellagio's lobby, heading down the shops arcade, into the crowded gaming rooms, toward the banks of elevators beneath ornate blown-glass chandeliers. It was business as usual in the ritzy hotel, and Lyman Zerga made as low-profile an entrance as was possible with bodyguards flanking him.

Virgil and Turk visually swept the area repeatedly as they crossed directly to the VIP concierge station at the near end of the front desk.

"Good afternoon, sir," the concierge said to the formidable new arrival. "How can I be of service?"

"My name is Lyman Zerga," Saul growled. "I'd like a suite please."

"Do you have a reservation with us?" the concierge asked haughtily, moving to his computer, ready to verify.

Lyman Zerga glared at him. "I don't make reservations."

A quick glance at Lyman's stolid bodyguards, as they too turned their blank-eyed dark glasses to stare at the concierge, told the functionary this was not a man to be denied. His fingers began to fly on the keyboard. He jumped to it.

FIFTEEN

The best restaurant in the Bellagio, the one situated just outside the entrance to the casino floor, had to be—by Terry Benedict's edict—the best restaurant in Las Vegas, if not the country. A tough mountain to climb: the Strip already had Emeril Lagasse and Wolfgang Puck.

But not tough if you think like Terry Benedict. How do you top the Hope diamond? You get two Hope diamonds.

The supreme Bellagio restaurant was run by not one highly sought-after media-celebrated chef, but two. Each one held court on alternating weeks. But their menus were available to diners every night—in the same restaurant.

Terry Benedict had made them offers they couldn't refuse: to be able to maintain their signature establishments in New York and LA, and at the same time work their culinary magic in Las Vegas. More kings than chefs, they reigned in the most lavishly equipped display kitchens ever designed, with huge staffs, no limits on food costs, and salaries so grand they almost embarrassed them.

Terry Benedict loved his twin culinary peaks. He loved the menu that changed practically by the hour. It was a rare night that he did not eat "at home."

Terry Benedict liked eating there. He liked that the menu that changed every day. He ate there nearly every night.

Rusty and Linus sat not far from the restaurant's entrance, in front of two slot machines. They idly dropped in quarters as they watched Lyman Zerga receiving the royal treatment at the hands of the VIP concierge and his uniformed minions. Mr. Zerga did not look impressed. He looked suitably impatient, a man with weighty and pressing international concerns.

"Okay," Rusty said to Linus as Saul and his entourage were whisked out of sight toward the elevator bay. "Tell me about Benedict."

"The guy is a machine," Linus said. He gave Rusty a rundown on his intelligence gathering about Benedict.

Linus had taken a close-up look at Vegas royalty: how they operate, how they are treated. Terry Benedict was the king of kings in Vegas— the royalest of the royals. A caesar.

Linus stationed himself near the Bellagio entrance and watched Benedict emerge from his town car. From his haircut to his smile to his crisp pant cuffs, he was effortless perfection. The king. Still he denied eye contact to no man.

"He arrives at the Bellagio everyday at two p.m.," Linus had reported to Rusty. "Same town-car, same driver. Remembers every valet's name on the way in. Not bad for a guy worth three-quarters of a billion."

Benedict strode into his casino, Linus stepped from behind a pillar and followed him in.

Benedict moved across the hotel lobby, smilingly greeting employees by name, glad-handing an occasional guest. He did not tarry long; he went straight to his private elevator and up to the second floor to work.

"Offices are upstairs," Linus reported to Rusty. "He works hard, hits the lobby floor at seven on the nose."

Watching from the craps table, Linus saw the private elevator doors open on the hotel lobby and Benedict step out. The great man strode into the casino and walked up onto the raised terrace, where the casino manager had his station. He stood overlooking the gaming floor, and within thirty seconds, the manager appeared beside him and they conferred.

"Spends three minutes on the floor with his casino manager," Linus reported.

"What do they talk about?" Rusty wanted to know.

"All business," Linus said. "Benedict likes to know what's going on in his casinos. Likes to be in control. There's rarely an incident he doesn't know about or handle personally."

Linus stayed close to Benedict and kept an ear, if

*not an eye, directly on him for the thirty minutes he
was on the floor working the room. He listened to him
speak to an Asian businessman in Cantonese, to a
Swiss visitor in German, and to some Italian visitors
in their halting English.*

"He spends a few minutes glad-handing the
high rollers," Linus reported. "He's fluent in
Spanish, German, and Italian, and he's taking
Japanese lessons, getting pretty good at it.

"He's out by seven-thirty," Linus went on,
"when an assistant hands him a black portfolio.
Contents: the day's take and new security codes.
Then he heads to the restaurant."

Rusty checked his watch as he and Linus continued their vigil at the slots with a view of the
restaurant entrance. They fed countless more
quarters in the machines and observed faithfully,
but no one entered.

"Give him another ten seconds," Linus said.

Around the corner came Benedict, carrying his
black portfolio.

"As I said, a machine," Linus said.

"And that portfolio contains the codes to all
the cage doors?" Rusty asked.

"Two minutes after they've been changed, he's
got 'em in hand."

They watched Benedict make his way toward
the restaurant, pausing for brief conversations
along the way.

"This guy is not just smart—he's ruthless,"
Linus said. "When Reuben refused his first offer

on the Paradiso, Benedict starved him out—cut off all his vendors, turned the unions against him, got him audited twice, hired away his lawyers. Reuben had no choice but to sell short. This guy doesn't go after your knees—he goes after your livelihood."

Benedict arrived at the restaurant entrance and stopped, checking his watch.

"Now comes the girl," Linus said, turning to the scene again. "If she comes in after he does, that means they're in a snit."

"Where's she come from?" Rusty said.

"The museum downstairs," Linus said. "She's the curator there. Wait. Here she is. You'll like this."

Rusty looked in the direction he nodded.

A stunning woman strode into view on lovely long legs. Elegantly dressed, doe-brown eyes, beautiful big smile—a knockout. She moved very much in her own private space. Heaven.

She was the same woman pictured in the background of the photograph of Terry Benedict that had appeared in the *New York Times*—the paper Danny saw in Atlantic City the day he got out.

Rusty's face just about dropped at the sight of her.

"I don't know if we can use her yet," Linus said. "I haven't even caught her name."

"Tess," Rusty said.

"What?" Linus said.

Rusty looked very certain about this, very certain and very upset. "Her name is Tess," Rusty said.

SIXTEEN

Construction was still going on in the wee hours in Tishkoff's warehouse. The guys were highly organized, keenly motivated. They had a goal. And it wasn't that far off. It was a simple goal: a pot of gold. But a pot big enough to buy a rainbow for each one of them.

A facsimile of the Bellagio vault was sprouting into shape. Livingston fixed a security camera in a corner, then found its image by framing Frank stapling floorboard into place, so that the area he now filmed matched a security tape of the real McCoy.

On the other side of the warehouse, Turk and Virgil were hard at work on their newly purchased vans with wrenches and blowtorches.

Tishkoff, wandering over to see how his money was being spent, recognized a gasket that Virgil was handling. "This looks familiar," Tishkoff said. "Where'd you get this?"

"Off your Rolls," Virgil said.

"Danny!" Tishkoff called. "Tell 'em not to touch the Rolls!"

Overlooking the whole enterprise, Danny grinned from ear to ear, happy at the progress. He waved Tishkoff off , busy checking a stopwatch in his hand, watching the stolen and modified casino cash cart sitting on the warehouse floor in front of him.

Sprang!

The false top to the cash cart flew open, revealing a human ball within, arms, legs, and torso folded into the confining three-by-four-foot space. The ball slowly unfolded into Yen, who whipped an air hose from his mouth and inhaled deeply.

Danny checked his stop watch. "29:47," he said. "Everything okay in there?"

Yen responded in his own language.

Of course, Danny didn't understand what he said. It was all Cantonese to him.

But Rusty, appearing behind Danny, understood. To Yen he said, "But what *doesn't* beat the shit out of being a circus performer?"

Danny turned, expecting to see Rusty grinning at his own joke. Instead he saw a Rusty who was looking very, very serious.

Outside, Rusty indicated.

Danny and Rusty adjourned from the warehouse.

"What is it?" Danny said.

"Tell me this isn't about her," Rusty said. "Or I'll walk off the job right now."

Danny looked at him blankly.

"Tess," Rusty said, off Danny's non-reaction. "She's with Terry Benedict now. Tell me this isn't about screwing the guy who's screwing your wife."

"Ex-wife," Danny said.

"Tell me," Rusty said.

"It's not. About that. Entirely."

Rusty stared at him levelly.

"You said you needed a reason," Danny said. "Well, this is mine."

Rusty just continued to give Danny more deadpan staring.

"When we started in this business," Danny said, "we had three rules. We weren't gonna hurt anybody. We weren't gonna steal from anybody who didn't have it coming. And we were gonna play the game like we had nothing to lose. Well, I lost something. Someone. That's why I'm here."

Rusty took a deep breath. "Here's the problem," he said. "We're stealing two things now. And when push comes to shove, if you can't have both, which are you gonna choose? And remember: Tess doesn't divide eleven ways."

The two men stood quietly looking at each other for a moment.

At last Danny said, "If things go to plan, I won't be the one who has to make that choice. How'd she look by the way?" Danny said. "Tess . . ."

"I've seen her happier," Rusty said.

SEVENTEEN

It was a real Picasso. *Woman with Guitar*.

"'Radiant' is the word," Tess said. "Absolutely radiant."

The painting hung in a place that would have to be termed an oxymoron—a most unlikely place: a casino art exhibit. Terry Benedict preferred to call it the Bellagio Hotel Art Gallery. In the world capital of neon, kitsch, and bad taste, where Western social and aesthetic values go to get turned on their heads, if not left out to die, an objet d'art of great beauty and worth had come to rest.

The painting hung under a portrait lamp on a wall between an equally real Van Gogh and a perfectly authentic Monet.

Two men stood in front of the painting, admiring it at a proper distance: the seller of the painting, a man by the name of Jean Santaniello, and the seller's aide-de-camp.

A Bellagio staff photographer and a handful of

other gallery and hotel personnel milled around nearby.

Off to the side, in a handsome blazer and a pleased smile, Tess stood transfixed by the painting. "He painted it in the summer of 1912," she said, "after the breakup with Fernande Olivier."

"She must have put him through hell," Mr. Santaniello said.

"You can see the conflict," Tess said. "He makes her both erotic and grotesque. He's hopelessly drawn to her, and yet she drives him crazy."

"Mr. Santaniello has an early flight," the aide-de-camp said, checking his watch. "Do you think Mr. Benedict will be late?"

"Mr. Benedict is never late," Tess said.

As if on cue, the double doors to the gallery swung open and Terry Benedict entered, right on time. He was elegant, beaming, commanding. All that was missing was the blare of trumpets announcing his arrival.

"Am I late?" Benedict said.

"Not at all, Mr. Benedict," Tess said, greeting him. "Allow me to introduce you to Mr. Jean Santaniello."

Benedict turned to the seller and said with a nod, "Mr. Santaniello, I apologize for keeping you. Mike Tyson was talking my ear off."

His joke was not lost on his listeners.

Mr. Santaniello smiled. "I understand it's going to be a hell of a fight," he said.

"We hope," Benedict said.

Tess beamed as she angled Benedict toward the painting. "Here it is," she said with a certain pride.

Benedict moved toward the painting, and as he did, he caught Tess in his glance, and his smile deepened. He looked at the painting. "Magnificant!" he said. "I've been following her for fifteen years now. At last I've made her a home."

He looked at Tess. "All the arrangements and so forth . . . ?"

"Done," Mr. Santaniello said. "She's yours."

"Not mine," Benedict said. "She belongs to everyone who comes into my hotel. Isn't that right, Ms. Ocean?"

"Yes, Mr. Benedict," Tess said.

"She's lovely, isn't she?" Benedict said without taking his eyes off Tess.

The seller was confused as to which woman Benedict referred—Tess or the subject of Picasso's masterpiece. Benedict specified the painting.

"I can't believe I was the only one who was after her," he said.

"You're the only one who met my price," Mr. Santaniello said.

"Ah, but this . . . You can't put a price on beauty," Benedict said. "But I shouldn't philosophize. I own casinos, after all."

"Can we get a quick shot?" the aide-de-camp said, holding up a camera. "Mr. Santaniello has a plane to catch."

Benedict gave Tess a quick look, and she took a step back. She understood she was not to be part of the photo.

Benedict and the seller posed together. *Flash!*

Transaction completed. Cachet transferred. Status authenticated.

Mr. Santaniello shook hands with Benedict and Tess and exited with his aide-de-camp in tow. The Bellagio factotums followed. Benedict remained, enthralled by the painting.

Tess moved up beside him. "You like it?" she said.

"I like that you like it," Benedict said.

A contemplative moment passed.

Then they went on to the next thing.

"I have some bad news from the world of high fashion," Benedict said, glancing Tess's way. "It seems that Mike Tyson will be wearing red on Saturday night. Red trunks with a white stripe."

"Oh?" Tess said.

"And you, as I recall, will be wearing a red Donna Karan?" Benedict said. "And when the TV camera picks us up in the front row, that red dress . . ."

"I see," Tess said, her face falling.

"He's a charming man," Benedict said, "but no one's going to be watching him when they can make a study of you." He smiled down at her. "I've asked Paolo to find three or four things for you to try. I hope you're not too disappointed."

She was, but she buried it.

"Are you sure?" Benedict said.

She nodded, and smiled faintly.

"I'll see you tonight," Benedict said.

Instinctively she leaned in to kiss him. He recoiled ever so slightly.

"What?" Tess said. "We're alone."

He let his eyes wander along the length of the ceiling, over all the eye-in-the-sky cameras hidden there.

She followed his look.

"In my hotels," Benedict said, "there's always someone watching." But he kissed her anyway.

"I'll see you tonight," Tess said.

He glanced once more at the Picasso as he moved away. "Actually, I do like it," Benedict said. Then he was gone . . . and the swinging doors swung shut.

Tess remained, looking at the closing doors, and the man who wasn't there. *He's rich. He's handsome and wooing. But am I happy?*

She wasn't even sure that was a relevant question.

She turned and looked at the Picasso. And startling comparisons between herself and the trophy painting popped to her mind. "Don't do it, Tess," she said to herself. "Don't get yourself all mental about this."

She brushed away the red-dress issue buzzing peskily around her head as she walked out.

EIGHTEEN

The High Rollers' Room was plush, brocaded, and acoustically insulated. It had none of the ambient buzz that filled the hoi polloi's gaming floor day and night. It was elegant, quiet, and tense.

At the single table in the corner that was operating, only the most minimal personal information had been exchanged among the players. The stakes had started high, mounted even higher, and were now approaching nosebleed level.

Scott Reinschmidt, the player in the first position, could afford it. A big, blond, athletic man, he'd been a pro golfer in the eighties. On the advice of a businessman partner in a pro-am, he'd put all his winnings into Microsoft, and now he gambled seriously and played golf only for fun.

In the second position, a man named Mr. Marcos Briano revealed little, saying only that he "came from money"—which apparently was the name of a country because he declined to claim

any other part of the world as home. He preferred to be called *Mister* Briano, thank you very
much.

Mr. Lyman Zerga, in the third position,
furtively peeled at his roll of Rolaids and slipped
one in his mouth.

"Weak stomach, Mr. Zerga?" the friendliest of
the high rollers said, a naturally curious man
named Tim Davis ("Call me Tim-o") who had
made his money as an accident-scam investiga-
tor for big insurance companies. Davis could
smell a scammer at a thousand yards, and he
smelled a hint of something about Zerga.

"I don't believe in weakness," Saul said, his
transformation into Zerga complete with an
unidentifiably accented voice. "It costs too
much. I don't believe in questions either."

That shut Tim-o up, at least for the moment.

Saul glanced up from the cards, just percepti-
bly, to spot Terry Benedict arriving on the floor,
right on schedule. He had chosen his seat and its
angle on the floor for just this reason: to be
ready.

Benedict approached the pit boss by the entrance. "Eddie," he said. "Anything for me?"

"Mr. Zerga, sir," the pit boss said, indicating
the high-roller room. "Lyman Zerga. In the third
position. Wishes to speak with you privately."

"Who is he?" Benedict said.

"Businessman of some kind, works mostly in
Europe," the pit boss said. "He's very vague, but

I asked around. Word is he deals primarily in arms. One of the biggest."

"Zerga?" Benedict said. "Never heard of him."

"Yes, sir," the pit boss said. "That's why I don't doubt it."

"He's staying here?" Benedict said.

"Checked in two nights ago, sir," the pit boss said. "He's in the Mirador Suite."

"How's he doing?" Benedict said.

"Up. Almost forty grand," said the pit boss.

"Good for him," Benedict said.

That sealed it. He couldn't duck a meet-and-greet with this Zerga, whoever he was. He had to make him feel that he was loved at the Bellagio, that they were honored by his presence. Zerga had too much of Benedict's money to be allowed to walk away soon.

The choicest booth inside the very best Bellagio restaurant was kept empty at all times, just in case. The "in cases" included Benedict himself, close friends sent in by Benedict, and of course Benedict's woman of the moment—the moment being an elastic unit of time that at present was stretching into something quite significant.

Tess Ocean sat in the booth, sipped a glass of wine, and checked her watch. The usually prompt Benedict was very close to being late.

A pair of hands slipped over her shoulders and started to caress her arms.

"You're thirty seconds late," Tess said without

looking at him. "I was about to send out a search party."

Looking down, recognizing the hands, she turned, stunned.

"Danny . . ." Tess said.

"Hello, Tess," Danny said, standing over her, grinning. Wondering what her reaction to seeing him would be. He saw it play out on her face.

Tess was thrilled and petrified and stunned to see him, but outraged mostly.

"What are you doing here?" she said.

"I'm out," Danny said.

"You're out," Tess said.

"Of prison," Danny said. "You remember? The day I went for cigarettes and never came back? You must have noticed."

"I don't smoke," Tess said as he sat. "Don't sit."

But he did. She knew he would. He was Danny Ocean, after all.

"They said I've paid my debt to society," he said.

"Funny, I never got a check," Tess said.

Danny smiled. Tess stared daggers.

"You can't stay," Tess said.

"It's good to see you," Danny said simultaneously. Without looking down at her hands, he said, "You're not wearing your ring."

An awkward moment of staring at each other passed.

"I sold it," Tess said. "And I don't have a husband. Or didn't you get the papers?"

"My last day inside," Danny said.

"I told you I'd write," Tess said.

Danny reached his hand, with its ring, for her ringless left hand, but she removed it from the table.

"Danny," Tess said. "Go. Now. Before . . ."

"Benedict?" Danny said.

She froze. Danny knew.

He smiled. It was okay. He signaled to a passing waiter. "Whiskey and"—he held his fingers two inches apart—"whiskey." He held his fingers one inch apart for Tess's drink.

"Danny," Tess said.

"You're doing a great job curating the museum," Danny said.

Tess sighed, exasperated.

"The Vermeer is quite good," Danny said. "Simple but vibrant. Although his work definitely fell off as he got older."

"Remind you of anyone?" Tess said.

"And I still get Monet and Manet confused," Danny said. "Which one married his mistress?"

"Monet," Tess said.

"Right," Danny said. "Manet had syphilis."

"They also painted occasionally," Tess said.

A beat passed.

"You don't know how many times I played this conversation out in my head the last two years," Danny said.

"Did it always go this poorly?" Tess said.

"Yes," Danny admitted with a smile.

"Sounds frustrating," Tess said.

"You were never easy," Danny said.

She shrugged. Not even a hint of a return smile. She was giving him nothing.

"Okay," Danny said. "I'll make this quick. I came here for you. I'm gonna get on with my life, and I want you with me."

"You're a thief and a liar," Tess said.

"I only lied about being a thief," Danny said. "But I don't do that anymore."

"Steal?" Tess said.

"Lie," Danny said.

"I'm with someone now who doesn't have to make that kind of distinction," Tess said.

"No," Danny said, "he's very clear on both."

"Nice," Tess said. "Work on that for two years too?"

"Year and a half," Danny said.

Finally, Danny was graced with a light smile from Tess. But that was all. "Do you know what your problem is?" she said.

"I only have one?" Danny said.

"You've met too many people like you," Tess said.

Danny looked at her, puzzling that one over.

"I'm with Terry now," Tess said.

"Does he make you laugh?" Danny asked.

"He doesn't make me cry," Tess said.

They weren't playing for matchsticks in the High Rollers' Room, and any possibility of the game relaxing into friendly banter had long since gone up in smoke.

The game now was blackjack. Saul held on a fourteen, facing the dealer's two.

Benedict approached, but seeing the status of the game, stopped and stood off to the right, watching.

The dealer revealed his down card—a five—then hit himself three times—a three, another five, and a queen.

"Dealer busts," the dealer said.

The dealer was Frank Catton.

Victorious but uncelebrating, Saul looked up. "Mr. Benedict," he said.

"Mr. Zerga," Benedict said.

"I recognize you from the TV," Saul said. "You know, nine casinos out of ten, the owner comes up in the middle of the hand to ask me what I want. I respect your waiting."

"You're the guest, sir," Benedict said.

"And I have to impose on your hospitality," Saul said. "Can you sit in for a hand?"

"I'd love to, Mr. Zerga, but the gaming board would feed me to my white tigers," Benedict said.

"That's a shame," Saul said. "You're the King of Vegas and you have to play craps in the alley."

"Not a shame at all," Benedict said. "Reminds me of my youth."

A few moments later, after Saul had cashed out of the game, he and Benedict were huddled in a corner, having a private exchange of great importance to "Mr. Zerga."

"The fight is Saturday," Saul said, "is it not?"

"Yes," Benedict said. "I can get you seats—"

"No, no," Saul said. "Hand-to-hand combat doesn't interest me. I have a package arriving here Saturday evening. A black briefcase, standard size, the contents of which are very valuable to me."

"I'd be happy to put it in the house safe for you," Benedict said.

"The house safe is for brandy and grandmother's pearls," Saul said. "I'm afraid I need something more secure."

"I can assure you," Benedict said, "the house safe is utterly—"

Saul's look stopped Benedict.

"I can assure you, Mr. Benedict, your generosity in this matter will not go overlooked," Saul said. "Now what can you offer me besides the safe?" Saul's eyes were pure steel. He was not a man familiar with being denied.

And Benedict recognized that fact.

The waiter had brought drinks and taken no money. It was Mr. Benedict's table and Mr. Benedict's woman, after all.

"See, the kind of people you steal things from," Tess said, "they have insurance to compensate them. They get made whole again. I had to leave New York to get away from what happened. How do I get my five years back, Danny?"

"You can't," Danny said. "But what you *can* do is not throw away another five years."

"You don't know anything about—" Tess said.

"Listen," Danny said, leaning in. "You don't love me anymore, you want to make a life with someone else? Fine. I'll have to live with that. But not him."

"Spoken like a true ex-husband," Tess said.

"I'm not joking, Tess," Danny said.

"I'm not laughing," Tess said. She sat glaring at him. "You have to admit there's a conflict of interest when you give me advice about my love life."

Danny exhaled and leaned back. "Yes," Danny said. "But that doesn't mean I'm wrong."

She looked at him, and maybe some part of her knew that he wasn't. She looked down at his ring, somewhat wistful.

He caught her looking at it.

"Do you remember what I said to you when we first met?" Tess said.

"You said, 'You better know what you're doing,'" Danny said.

"Do you? Now?" Tess said. "Because—truly—you should walk out the door if you don't."

"I know what I'm doing," Danny said, not entirely sure why she brought it up.

"What are you doing?" Benedict said.

Now Danny knew. He looked up.

Terry Benedict was hovering over them, fresh from his meeting with Saul.

"Catching up," Danny said.

"Terry," Tess said, "meet my ex-husband."

"Danny Ocean," Danny said, extending his hand.

"Mr. Ocean," Benedict said, shaking with Danny.

"Forgive me for being late," Benedict said to Tess. "A guest required my attention."

"Danny was just walking through the restaurant and spotted me," Tess explained.

"Is that right?" Benedict said.

"I was shocked myself," Danny said. "Imagine the odds."

"'Of all the gin joints in all the world,'" Benedict said.

Silence. Not awkward, just mutually appraising alpha males circling each other.

"You've been in prison until recently—isn't that right?" Benedict said. "How does it feel to be out?"

"About the same," Danny said. "Everything you want is still on the other side."

"There's the human condition for you," Benedict said.

"Terry," Tess said, "Danny was just about to—"

"I just wanted to say hello," Danny interrupted, "for old times' sake."

"Stay for a drink, if you like," Benedict said.

"He can't," Tess said.

"I can't," Danny agreed.

Another silence. This time it was awkward. Danny was still sitting across from Tess. Benedict was still standing.

Benedict solved the problem his way. He

staked his claim by taking Tess's hand in his.
"Well, then," he said, "I don't imagine we'll be
seeing you again, Mr. Ocean."

"You never know," Danny said.

"I know everything that happens in my hotels," Benedict said.

"So I should put those towels back," Danny
said.

"The *towels* you can keep," Benedict said.

Danny smiled and rose from the table at last.

"Good seeing you, Tess," Danny said.

"Take care, Danny," Tess said.

Danny walked away.

She waited until he was out the door and
gone. "I'm sorry," she said.

"Don't be," Benedict said like lightning.

Tess noticed a chill in the air.

NINETEEN

Exiting the restaurant into the Bellagio lobby, Danny caught himself snapping his fingers. He'd seen a mist in Tess's eyes, and he knew he had a fighting chance with her. He was convinced. It was not over.

What he did not know was that Linus was tailing him, ten steps back. Linus, his own teammate, one of Ocean's Eleven. Linus stopped, glanced back at the restaurant quizzically, then continued following Danny.

Basher Tarr's hotel room was not a place to light a match. The place was a powder keg. Surrounded by combustibles, Basher sat on his bed, whittling and polishing a plastic explosive into the shape of a jewel with the polished hues of an emerald.

A knock resounded at the door.

"Housecleaning," a maid said outside in the hall.

"Just jumping into the shower," Basher said, his eyes never leaving his work. "Can you come back later?"

The maid moved on.

On Basher's TV, the local news was live from the Strip, covering a much-anticipated event.

Sandy Margolis was a star in her own right. The popular anchor for a Las Vegas network affiliate was front and center, lending her own bit of glamour to what was being touted as a landmark occasion.

"We're here at the historic Paradiso Hotel and Casino," Margolis said, broadcasting live from the middle of a throng of spectators. "Once the prize resort of Las Vegas, it is now seconds away from demolition."

The pleasantly plump Margolis hopped nimbly up on the temporary dais that had been raised for this paradoxically festive occasion and, amid cheers and friendly yells, took her place at the microphone as official announcer.

The simply curious had gathered, along with a few closet anarchists and would-be mad bombers. Great acts of destruction, like train wrecks or public hangings, always draw a crowd. The clock ticked down on Reuben Tishkoff's bankrupt hotel's few remaining moments, while local luminaries posed before the cameras and made ready.

The proud but, by comparison, old-fashioned Paradiso stood just down the block from the newer, sleeker, more resplendent trio of Benedict hotel casinos: the Mirage, the Bellagio, and the MGM Grand. All of which were lit up gloriously for a party, while the old-girl Paradiso had not so much as a sparkle of light or life left in her.

Terry Benedict reigned at the center of the dais, the lead figure whose forefinger would press the button. He was surrounded by the mayor of Las Vegas, a Nevada Congressman, local council people, and various other officials, among them the powerful sheriff of Clark County, on whose good side all the potentates of Sin City took pains to be.

Tess was on the dais too, standing near her man.

Buried in the crowd below the dais, hidden within the masses, was Danny, who only had eyes for his ex.

Linus lurked nearby, keeping a steady bead on Danny.

"And here's Reuben Tishkoff," Margolis said, "former owner of the Paradiso, come to bid farewell to his fabled resort and wish Terry Benedict all the best with his future plans for the property."

Reuben stepped forward and Benedict greeted him before the TV cameras and still photographers. Everyone was smiling and shaking hands.

But behind those smiles and under their breath, the weather was far from sunny.

"Good to see you," Benedict said.

"Go shit in your mouth," Reuben said.

Tess, her eyes roaming the crowd, found a pair of eyes staring back at her off to one side: Danny's. He acknowledged. She held his glance a long beat.

Long enough for Benedict to notice, though her head was turned away from him at this significant moment.

Further back in the crowd, Linus noted the exchange too.

Tess turned back to Benedict just as he put his public smile back on and stepped up to the microphone alongside Mike Tyson and Lennox Lewis. The two boxers and Benedict all put their hands on the plunger.

Benedict leaned into the microphone. "I hope there's as much dynamite in the Paradiso as there will be in this Saturday's fight," Benedict said.

The crowd roared its approval and the three men plunged the plunger. *Whoomph!* The Paradiso imploded quite grandly, thundering to the earth in a cascade of steel and brick and plaster, sending a rising mushroom of dust and smoke high into the air.

Reuben wiped a tear from his eye. "G'bye, honey," he said.

Basher would not even have looked up at the roar and rumble of the Paradiso's demise, just a few hundred yards up the Strip from his hotel room, but for the annoying fact that the lights and TV in his room flickered and went out.

"Shit," Basher said. He had a bad feeling about this.

He abandoned his labors and scrambled out the door, making sure to post a DO NOT DISTURB sign on the outside knob as he went.

Basher was AWOL when the crew met in Tishkoff's game room that evening. "Saturday is yours," Rusty said. "Do whatever you like with it."

But for now, he warned, it was business of the highest importance.

Ocean's Eleven minus one surrounded the cut-away model of the Strip and the three casinos as Rusty led everyone through a minute-by-minute rundown of the heist.

"Call is at five-thirty," Rusty said. "Makeup and costumes. Saul's package arrives at seven-fifteen, and Linus grabs our codes. All goes well there and we're a go. Seven-thirty Virgil and Turk deliver Yen, and we're committed. From that point, we have thirty minutes to blow the power or he suffocates."

They all stared down at their holy grail—the miniature of the vault.

"Once the electricity goes," Rusty said, "all entry points to the vault and its elevator will automatically lock down for two minutes. That's when we make our move. . . ."

At the full-size Bellagio vault, the real-deal, a clock read 8:03 P.M. The heavy door swung open.

Two guards wheeled in a cash cart, left it in the vault's center, and marched out again, closing the thick metal door behind them.

Then the vault locks clicked.

There was silence for a spell, the lights flickered out, and . . .

. . . the false top of the cart sprung open, revealing Yen within, folded neatly. He inhaled deeply, then slowly unspooled himself from the cash cart until, at last, he crouched atop it. He took in the silent and vacant room.

Rusty walked right by Yen, incongruously, while the rest of the team, who were in the warehouse, stood around the Bellagio vault, which they had fully reproduced there.

What they were watching was a trial run.

"Okay, they've put you in the middle of the room far from everything," Rusty said to Yen. "You have to get from here to the door without touching the floor. What do you do?"

The rest of the eleven who weren't onstage—except Basher, who was still missing—watched as if they were a film crew watching a dress rehearsal.

"Fin says he shorts it," Frank said.

"Make it a sawbuck," Livingston said.

From a dead squat, Yen leapt, hands first, from the cash cart toward a ledge five yards away. With hands and fingers outspread, he gripped the ledge safely with both hands without touching the floor. From this position, he meticulously inched his way to a counter, and then to the door.

Frank paid up.

Behind him, a door slammed, and they turned to see Basher, at last.

They did double takes, sniffing the air. Basher was covered from head to toe in sewage.

And he wasn't happy.

He was the bearer of bad, and smelly, news.

"We're in deep shit," Basher said.

In the farthest corner of the warehouse, Linus hosed his stinking colleague off.

Basher, his Limey accent angry and thick, spit out fetid water and the story of his afternoon. And if nobody understood a word he was saying, that was okay. They certainly got the general drift.

"The damn demo crew didn't use a coaxial lynch to back the mainline!" Basher said. "Onioned the mainframe couplet!"

The demolition crew at the Paradiso obviously had done something wrong in the electrical hookup they'd rigged.

Reuben leaned into Livingston. "You understand any of this?"

"I'll explain later," Livingston said.

"Blew the backup grid one by one! Like dominoes!" Basher said

"Basher," Danny said because he hardly understood this either, "what happened?"

Basher had gone back into the sewers to find

out what had caused the blackout, and he'd come upon a platoon of city engineers doing their own investigation. They were examining the complex of subterranean fuse boxes, and Basher tailed them, hiding near a waterfall of effluent.

"The bloody demos did exactly what I planned to do," Basher said. "Only they did it by accident. Now they know their weakness. And they're fixing it."

It was a setback—if not a brick wall—that threatened to stop the project altogether.

But the bath of ordure? How did Basher get dunked in the sewer?

A footstep that echoed was all it took, Basher sourly explained. The city engineers' ears had perked up, and Basher had had to retreat into the excremental waterfall to hide.

As he toweled off his hair later in Tishkoff's living room, Basher made it clear that his scheme for knocking out the flow of power to the Strip was kaput. It just wouldn't work now. The engineers were busy, even as they spoke, building redundancies into the power system choke point that Basher had figured a way to squeeze shut.

"So . . . ?" Danny said.

"So unless we decide to do this job in Reno, we're screwed," Basher said.

Danny rose and paced, frustrated. He'd come too far for things to go awry now. "We could—" Danny started.

"By tomorrow?" Rusty said.

Danny kept pacing.

Rusty hung his head and thought.

Basher dried his hair. And as he finished, an idea occurred to him. "We could use a pinch," Basher said.

Danny stopped. Rusty looked up.

"What," Danny asked, "is a pinch?"

As Basher explained to his less technologically literate associates, the pinch he had in mind—a pinch the size they'd need—was a lithium wire in a glass vacuum tube the size of a small refrigerator.

"A pinch," he said, "is the equivalent of a cardiac arrest for any broad-band electrical circuitry."

So far they understood.

"Or better yet," he said, "a pinch is a bomb . . . but without the bomb. Every time a nuclear weapon detonates, it unleashes an electromagnetic pulse that shuts down any power source within its vicinity. That tends not to matter in most cases because the nuclear weapon destroys everything you might need power for anyway. Now a pinch creates a similar electromagnetic pulse, but without the headache of mass destruction and death. So instead of Hiroshima, you get the seventeenth century."

Got it.

A tube that zaps electric power sources to a standstill.

"For how long?" Rusty said.

"About ten seconds," Basher said.

"Could a pinch take out the power of an entire city?" Danny said.

"Las Vegas?" Basher said with a smile.

They all looked at him with hope.

"But there's only one pinch in the world big enough to handle it," Basher said.

Danny and Rusty traded a look. They had their answer.

"Where?"Danny said.

Basher hated to say this. "Pasadena," he said balefully.

TWENTY

Cal Tech wasn't that far from Vegas. A few hours' drive at breakneck speeds through the Nevada Desert, then the Mojave Desert of Southern California, then over some mountains, in the dark of night.

With Turk at the wheel, Virgil riding shotgun, the white van carried more than half the team on a make-or-break mission. Six men out to pinch a pinch.

The van spanned the deserts, then sped up and over the San Gabriel Mountains and down into the leafy environs of Pasadena—home to one of the brain-cell powerhouses of the Western world.

This was the place where they were building the next generation of hyperefficient, inside-out rocket engines for the space shuttle. Where they were designing and trying to figure out how to test a thinner-than-paper, three-mile-wide solar sail to power a spacecraft at seventeen thousand miles per second to planets in the next star system.

The symbiotically combined organism of the California Institute of Technology and NASA, with its fabulous, government-enhanced budget, was busy creating the future of technological wizardry and inventing uses for it as it went along. What possible practical use would there be for a refrigerator-sized pinch? the appropriations committee at the University wanted to know.

You never know, was the scientists' answer.

Good enough, said the committee. Approved. Next . . .

Danny, Basher, Yen, and Linus huddled in the back watching as Basher and Yen both prepared equipment for their raid: hooks and a rope for Yen, a small blowtorch and a drill for Basher.

The guard kiosk at the Cal Tech front gate was manned by a magazine-reading graduate student. The white van cruised along farther and turned down a side street and onto the campus.

The headlights hit a sign:

CAL TECH

HIGH-SECURITY AREA

KEEP OUT.

The van shot past it.

"You two ready?" Danny said to Basher and Yen.

They nodded and, with Danny in the lead, started out the van's rear door.

When Linus started to follow, Danny said, "What are you doing?"

"Coming with you," Linus said.

Danny smiled and shook his head.

"But . . ." Linus said, furious.

The van door slammed in his face. Linus sat staring at the closed door in disbelief.

The exterior door at the high-security laboratory was, by casino or bank standards, a joke. Using a standard lock-pick technique, Danny clicked it open within fifteen seconds. So much for breaching the perimeter defenses of the U.S. military-industrial-academic complex.

Danny, Yen, and Basher disappeared into the lab's interior with their minimalist set of tools.

Their footsteps echoed loudly. No guards patrolled the halls. By the empty look of things, their greatest danger would come from some Cal Techno nerd who was pulling an all-nighter using the labs megacomputers to try to take pi out to enough decimal places to make it come out even.

Back in the white van, Linus twiddled his thumbs, sick to death of being seated at the kiddie table.

In the front seat, no such problem. Another Mensa meeting had been called to order.

"Are you a man?" Virgil said.

"Yes," Turk said, counting off the number of questions Virgil had asked him. "Nineteen."

"Are you alive?" Virgil said.

"Yes," Turk said. "Eighteen."

"Evel Knievel," Virgil said.

"Shit!" Turk said. "Okay, your turn."

Twenty rounds of Twenty Questions later, the game changed to astrophysics.

"Cosine squared over .0455," Virgil said.

"No," Turk said. "Cosine squared over .0415."

".04-5-5," Virgil said.

"One-5," Turk said.

"You're so wrong," Virgil said.

"You don't know your string theory, bitch," Turk said.

They then did twenty-six games of Here's-the-First-Line/Name-the-Work-and-Author. Then a rousing new game of Describe-the-Crime/Name-the-Serial-Killer. Then a timed game of world capitals . . . whereupon they started to get bored and suddenly fell silent.

Linus, courting insanity in the back of the van, thanked the heavens.

After a spell of silence, Virgil said quietly, "Mom told me she loves me more."

"She told me she was going to tell you that," Turk said.

Linus just closed his eyes.

"Stop it," Turk said.

"Make me," Virgil said.

"Stop it," Turk said.

"Make me," Virgil said.

With his eyes still closed, Linus heard the two oafish brothers, incredibly, wrestling in the front of the van. That was enough. He opened his eyes, cracked the back door, checked up front, and sneaked out without the Malloys hearing him.

Linus jogged along the laboratory's perimeter, checking doors, until he found the one whose lock Danny had picked. He looked back at the van and disappeared inside.

Not twenty seconds later, the next door down opened, and Danny, Basher, and Yen appeared, pinch in hand. They'd succeeded. They wove a path to the van, carrying the delicate, bulky instrument.

Turk and Virgil were still wrestling as the trio appeared. Danny, Basher, and Yen piled in the back with their prize and hurriedly bundled it in blankets.

"We got it," Danny said. "Let's go."

Turk straightened up and floored it, and they were off.

"Wait a minute," Danny called out.

Turk braked, and they weren't off after all.

"Where's Linus?" Danny said.

He wasn't there, and everyone finally realized it.

Just then, sirens and alarms and lights came to life. Uh-oh.

Danny spun around to look out the back of the van. Basher by his side, they scanned the darkened compound through the window.

"There he is," Danny said. He pointed to the

now-lit, see-through beveled-glass stairwell inside the lab.

Linus scrambled up its steps, a flight ahead of a pair of chasing guards. He ascended out of sight, heading toward the roof level.

Danny, Yen, and Basher squatted at the back windows and watched as, on the other side of the building, two more guards arrived on the roof and moved toward the central staircase. Linus would be trapped.

Yen gestured and made a colorful observation about Linus's predicament, which, of course, no one understood.

None of them made a move to go to Linus's aid.

Finally Virgil said, "One of us should help him."

"Then there'll be two of us who need saving," Basher said, speaking Danny's mind.

"He knows where we are," Danny said.

Now the first pair of guards emerged from the stairwell onto the rooftop to join the second pair. They found no Linus between them. He'd disappeared.

"Where'd he go?" Turk said.

Danny and Basher, realizing they were hearing both brothers' voices just inches behind them, slowly turned. Both Turk and Virgil were crouched just inches behind them. Well, they wanted to spectate as well.

"What?" Turk said, off Danny's exasperated look.

Then, *bong!* It occurred to Turk. He turned to his brother. "Would you—shouldn't someone be behind the wheel?"

Suddenly, the sound of shattering glass filled the night.

A second-story window in the Cal Tech lab exploded as a desk chair flew through it, followed shortly by Linus, who leapt onto a steel-mesh overhang running alongside the building.

"All right, back it up, back it up!" Danny said.

Virgil dove into the driver's seat and slammed it into reverse. He snaked the van backward to the side of the lab.

Linus ran along the overhang, while behind him, two guards climbed out after him and started along the wire mesh. Linus came to the end of the structure and leapt. He came crashing down onto the reversing van, then rolled along its roof and down its windshield.

Through the windshield, Virgil got his attention and jabbed his thumb over his shoulder—get in the back.

"C'mon, c'mon!" Danny yelled to him, sticking his head above the rear doors.

Linus scrambled back over the roof of the van, went on his belly, and let Danny and Yen flip him down and pull him through the rear doors. Virgil hit the gas for a quick getaway, but he did so before the rear doors were closed. One of them rebounded and slammed shut right on Yen's hand—*crunch!*

"Ahhhhh!" Yen yelled out in a language they all clearly understood.

As the white van hurtled away, Basher tended to Yen, examining his hand, cradling it, struck with a sense of foreboding. Yen's performance was key to the whole operation, and Yen's two hands were key to his performance.

Yen remained stoically silent, but he was white with pain.

Danny stared down at Linus, who lay panting and breathless on the floor of the van. "I say, 'stay in the van,' you stay in the van," Danny said. "Got it? 'Cause you lose focus for one second in this game, and someone gets hurt."

"I got it," Linus said, but without remorse. He lurched to a sitting position and backed against the wall of the van. Though he did feel bad for Yen's hand, he'd had just about enough of Danny's shit.

They continued staring daggers at one another as the van sped away into the night.

With any luck, thought Danny, the guards would think Linus was a prank-playing Stanford student, jealous of Cal Tech's bigger linear accelerator. They wouldn't notice the missing pinch until Monday morning, well after it had—or had not—served its useful purpose for the Ocean cabal.

TWENTY-ONE

"It's fight night in Las Vegas," said sportscaster Jim Lampley in his radio feed, picked up by the boys in the van, motoring up I-15 into the big town the next day.

Motoring slowly.

Incoming lanes of the interstate reflected bumper-to-bumper steel: cars, trucks, SUVs, RVs, and charter buses. Planes in the air were stacked for five miles over the desert: jumbos, sleek business jets, prop-driven two-seaters.

A big fight night brought all kinds to Las Vegas.

Fans, of course.

Grifters, scammers and pickpockets, too.

As well as golf hustlers, poker hustlers, and ticket scalpers, and out-of-town working girls and their pimps.

These out-of-town sex poachers were the bane of the local working girls, who had homes in Vegas and regular lives and a steady business on the Strip. The much-loathed visiting hookers trooped in from Dallas, New Orleans, Atlanta, and Miami, hoping to skim the cream off the top of the fight-night big spenders. Turf spats and hair pulling were to be expected.

Even the Gila monsters out in the desert seemed Vegas-bound.

"People are flooding in from all over the country," said Jim Lampley, "to see what has been dubbed the 'Fight to End All Fights.'"

Lampley was set up in the boiling Vegas sun, doing his broadcast live from a mobbed Strip. "And even though it's still five hours till the opening bell," he reported, "the energy here is fever-pitched."

Adults milled around the Strip like teenagers, cruising, shmoozing, gawking, trolling—like college kids on spring break.

On the Bellagio's gaming floor, every table was in play, every seat filled.

In the Bellagio security center—the Eye in the Sky—Terry Benedict's senior casino manager, the one who Linus watched briefing Benedict each night, checked in with his watchers. "How are we doing?" he said.

There would be incredibly high volume this night, high expectations for a huge-grossing weekend. It was no time for lapses or screwups of any kind. Any snafu could cost the casino millions—and would cost any slacker his job.

"How are we doing?"

There was only one acceptable answer.

Only the highest of high rollers were swaddled in the Mirador Suite at the Bellagio, the lap-of-luxury suite in a hotel that prided itself on obscene extravagance. It was where Donald Trump stayed when he came on a busman's holiday. It was where the Supreme Emir of the United Arab Emirates crashed when he was passing through. It was where the VIP concierge had put Lyman Zerga, little-known but powerful arms dealer from trans-Europe.

Dell Livingston, little-known electronic-surveillance genius from LA, had moved his audio-visual operations into Lyman Zerga's suite.

The "spider" that Livingston had planted on the downstairs communications ganglion was beaming the casino's big picture up to the Ocean team.

As he scoured the exact same images the gaming-floor and security watchers downstairs were watching, he eavesdropped on their communications through his headset.

"Cotton couldn't be taller," the watcher said over Livingston's headset. The watcher was looking out on a gambling floor that was wall to wall people, yacking, drinking, throwing money down on the green felt, and laughing up a storm.

In the Mirador bathroom—lost in the opulence his role dictated—Saul floated in the full-size Jacuzzi and chewed on a hundred-dollar cigar.

Relaxation was his middle name. It was his way of getting ready to go on.

Reuben, meanwhile, paced the floor like a hungry chicken waiting for feed call.

"Where are they?" Reuben said. "That's what I want to know. Where are they?"

"They'll be here," Saul said in full Lyman voice and character.

"'They'll be here,'" Reuben said to himself, mocking Saul. "Thanks a lot, Fidel."

Livingston, at his console, was punching up a new set of views from the Eye in the Sky, covering the waterfront, keeping tabs on the casino's whole operation.

"Yikes," he said, thrusting forward. The new view on the screen got his attention in a big way.

Rusty waited downstairs in the Bellagio hotel lobby, keeping watch on the hotel's side entrance. He glanced at his watch, then outside again. He had every faith the boys would make it back on time and in one piece.

He looked at his watch again, and it had only moved one minute since he checked it last. He was racked with doubt. It was over. They had failed. It was all a pipe dream. The whole operation was a flimsy house of cards.

The white van pulled up at the side entrance and dropped off Linus and Danny, who slapped the van's roof and watched it pull away with both Malloys and Yen.

Danny and Linus entered the lobby, and Rusty,

now flush with good feelings about the whole beautiful operation, fell into step with them. He exchanged a smile with Danny but got nothing from Linus—who looked tight, stone-faced.

In the elevator riding up, Rusty looked the two men over. "You boys have a nice trip?" he said. Smiling, he looked at Linus, who glowered. Then at Danny, who was about to explain, but the doors parted at the Mirador Suite.

Livingston greeted them urgently, waving them over to his monitor. "We have a problem," he said.

They stepped around all the equipment to the screen Livingston pointed out and looked.

On Livingston's laptop was a mug shot of Danny, complete with vital information: height, weight, and criminal history.

"You've been red-flagged," Livingston said. "It means the moment you step on the casino floor, they'll be watching you. Like hawks. Hawks with video cameras."

"This is a problem," Danny said.

A pall fell over the room. This was more than a problem—this was disastrous, yet another bump in an endless procession of potholes on the road to over $150 million. Only Saul, unaware, dared to make a noise, humming and splashing away in the next room.

"Saul, time to get out," Rusty said.

"It's time when I say it is," Saul said in Lyman character.

"Now!" Rusty said.

They heard Saul jump immediately out of the tub.

"I'm out," Saul said, himself again.

"You have any idea how this happened?" Rusty said back to Danny.

Before Danny could answer, Linus cracked, "I do." Looking at Danny with no love lost, he said, "He's been chasing Benedict's woman. Got into a real snarl with him two nights ago."

Danny stared at him.

"I was tailing you," Linus said.

"Who told you to do that?" Danny said.

Before Linus could answer, Rusty said, "I did."

He and Danny held a stare.

"I knew you couldn't leave Tess alone," Rusty said.

"Who's Tess?" Reuben said.

"My wife," Danny said.

"Ex-wife," Rusty said.

"Tess is here?" Saul said, appearing in a bathrobe.

Rusty's eyes were still on Danny. "I'm sorry," he said. "I didn't know if it would sting you, but it did."

He looked down at the red-flag photo of Danny on the computer terminal, then back up at his friend.

"You're out, Danny," Rusty said—the most difficult words he'd ever had to say.

"He's out?" Reuben said.

"It's that or we shut down right now," Rusty said. "His involvement puts us all at risk."

Danny and Rusty faced off, nose to nose, furious with each other.

"This isn't your call," Danny growled.

"You made it my call," Rusty said, "when you put her ahead of us."

"This is my job," Danny said.

"Not anymore," Rusty said.

Danny glowered at Rusty, then stepped back and looked around the room. One by one, he could see, everyone was going over to Rusty's side. It was the only way.

Defeated, he turned away and stalked out of the room—out onto the balcony, but not without raking Linus with a cold stare as he went.

"But, but . . . he can't just be out," Reuben said. "Who's gonna take his place?"

Rusty turned to Linus.

"Kid, you up for it?" Rusty said.

Linus's eyes drifted to Danny outside—whatever acrimony he'd felt before, he never meant to kick Danny off the job. He nodded, half cocksure, half scared pissless. He was up for it.

"Find everyone else," Rusty said to Livingston. "Let 'em know the change in plan. Curtain goes up at seven."

Livingston exited.

Everyone else in the room staggered about, like witnesses after an execution.

Linus watched Rusty step out onto the balcony—perhaps to console Danny—but from inside, their words could not be heard.

"Tess is with Benedict now?" Saul asked the room.

Nobody responded.

"She's too tall for him," Saul said.

TWENTY-TWO

In the dressing room of Terry Benedict's own royal suite at the Bellagio, Tess Ocean was readying herself for the big evening. She dressed up well, she'd been told, though this time it was not to be in Donna Karan red. As she fastened on an earring, she met her own glance in a dressing mirror, then caught sight of Benedict in the same reflection, pacing the bedroom behind her.

"Yes," Benedict said into the phone. "Yes. No. Very much no."

He then listened for a long moment.

"Then inform Mr. Levin he'll find a better view of the fight in front of his television," Benedict said. "Surely he must have HBO."

Hanging up, Benedict allowed himself a good chortle at his own joke. He approached Tess and put his hands on her shoulders. "What are you thinking about?" Benedict said.

"You," Tess said. She smiled at him in the mirror.

His glance turned from her to himself, appraising and admiring his polished reflection.

The couple did not speak as the executive elevator purred downward. Tess wore her trademark faint smile. Benedict stared straight ahead, lost in some inner calculation.

As they neared the main floor, he checked his watch. The elevator doors swooshed open and they stepped out into the casino: the King of Las Vegas and his consort.

The time was 7:00 P.M. on the dot.

Leaving Tess with a cocktail in the restaurant lounge, Benedict moved smoothly up to the low balcony overlooking the casino floor to meet his casino manager, precisely according to schedule, the special night notwithstanding.

"Any sign of Ocean?" Benedict said.

"Not in a couple hours," Walsh, the manager, said. "You want him out? I can bounce him from the state for parole violation if you like."

Benedict shook his head. "Put someone on him," he said. "He's here for a reason. I'd like to know what it is." He gazed thoughtfully across the packed casino floor. "But if he comes anywhere near Tess, take it to the next level."

"Bruiser?" the manager said.

Benedict nodded and stepped down off the balcony to take care of one more piece of business before retrieving Tess and beginning the evening's gala entertainment.

*   *   *

At the exterior entrance to the casino, Lyman Zerga, aka Saul Bloom, stood ramrod straight, looking through sliding-glass doors out at the valet station, like a man awaiting his destiny.

From behind him, Terry Benedict approached, accompanied by two blazered security guards walking half a pace behind.

Saul spotted him in the glass's reflection; he did not turn. "Mr. Benedict," Saul growled in his vaguely foreign accent.

"Mr. Zerga," Benedict said. "It's a very busy night for me. Are we on schedule?"

"I have no reason to suspect otherwise," Saul said, his eyes still straight ahead. "My couriers should be here momentarily."

A moment passed as Benedict studied the enigmatic older man. "It's a nice evening," Benedict said. "Shall we wait outside?" Zerga nodded.

Benedict and Saul emerged into the Bellagio's valet area just outside the doors, with Benedict's two bodyguards positioned on their flanks. The sun was setting over the Strip, and the temperature had already fallen to eighty-three degrees.

From a distance, a pair of binoculars picked out the two men immediately.

Upstairs, another part of the Ocean team was waiting, constantly checking the time.

"They're in position." Turk's voice came over

the headset wrapped around Livingston's sweat-drenched head.

"Okay. We're a go," Livingston said over static as he watched events unfold on his monitors.

Idling in traffic a few hundred feet down from the entrance to the Bellagio's grand driveway, an unmarked white van suddenly accelerated. It turned into the Bellagio's huge circular driveway and raced up to the curb where Mr. Lyman Zerga and Terry Benedict waited.

Turk Malloy swiftly dismounted from the passenger's side, a briefcase handcuffed to his wrist. Virgil came around from the driver's side, both of them dressed in their bodyguard suits.

"Mr. Zerga," Turk said as he approached. "A gift from Mr. Hesse."

Turk extended the briefcase to Zerga, and Zerga grasped the handle, but without trying to take possession. As both men clasped the handle simultaneously, Virgil produced a key, unlocked the cuff on Turk's wrist, transferred it to Mr. Zerga's, clamped it shut, and handed the older man the key.

"Thank you, Friedrich, Gunther," Zerga said.

He turned and nodded to Benedict. Then they retreated into the hotel, Zerga firmly in possession of the valued briefcase.

Benedict's security guards flanked the two men as they went in, and the Malloys entered right along with them, keeping pace. They marched in phalanx style back through the crowded floor of the gaming room, a guard on each corner.

In the Bellagio blackjack bay, Frank Catton dealt blackjack to a full table, with a waiting line. The energy and the mood of the gamblers were high; they were betting fast and aggressively. Frank was dealing just as fast and smoothly, keeping the game at a brisk and lucrative tempo.

As he laid down a new round of cards, his eyes gazed past his players to an entourage passing by: Mr. Lyman Zerga, the four guards, and Benedict, heading toward the cage.

"Lookin' like a bad night for the house," Frank said to no one in particular as he busted.

Chuckles bubbled up from the happy gamblers.

Terry Benedict, always working, always scanning, saw something out of the corner of his eye he didn't want to see: Danny Ocean lurking at a slot machine.

Without turning his head, Benedict said to one of his guards, "Find Mr. Walsh. Tell him Mr. Ocean's in the west slots."

The guard went, and Benedict continued with Saul. "I'm afraid I can't allow any private-security personnel inside the casino cages," he said. "I hope you don't mind."

"Of course not," Zerga said.

He turned to dismiss Virgil and Turk when, passing by on his way to a sports betting window, an old Miami racetrack denizen by the name of Buchanan happened past the group. Worse yet, happened to recognize Saul.

A friendly guy with the natural urge to connect, Buchanan reached out. "Saul?" he said. "Saul Bloom, is that you?"

Saul did his best to ignore the man. But even Benedict noticed this guy seemed to know Lyman Zerga—but by a different name.

"Saul, it's me!" the guy persisted. "Bucky Buchanan, remember? From Saratoga."

At last, with eyes as cold and emotionless as a shark, Saul turned to face this man. "Friedrich, Gunther," Lyman Zerga said in full accent.

He nodded a curt order: dispose of this man.

Virgil and Turk picked up Bucky Buchanan by his elbows and hauled him away.

"Mr. Benedict," Saul said. He gestured to the cage, then to his briefcase cuff. "Please. I have never enjoyed the touch of steel to my skin."

They proceeded at a brisk pace towards the Bellagio's cages.

At the west slots, Danny perched on the edge of a high stool in a row of octogenarians, all vacantly dropping dollar coins and pulling levers.

He dropped a dollar in his slot, watching out of his peripheral vision as Saul and Benedict disappeared into the money cage.

Ding! Ding! Ding! Ding!

Four cherries.

Danny smiled, a big winner.

But mostly a good omen. He had bigger pots to win tonight. He steered a neighboring senior citizen, who was blind as a bat, to the slot machine.

"Pops, you won," Danny said. Then he slipped away.

TWENTY-THREE

Linus stood before the dressing mirror in the Mirador Suite, dressed in a sharp, well-fitted conservative suit—a far cry from the nondescript street-threads thief in the subways of Chicago.

Rusty circled him, inspecting. "Where you gonna put your hands?" he said.

Linus clasped his hands in front of him.

"No," Rusty said.

Linus went for his pockets.

"Not the pockets either," Rusty said. "And don't touch your tie. Look at me."

Linus did.

"How you gonna stand?" Rusty said

Linus shifted his balance.

"Wrong again," Rusty said. "I ask you a question, you have to think of the answer. Where you gonna look?"

Linus looked down.

"Death," Rusty said. "You look down, they know you're lying."

Linus looked up.

"And up they know you don't know the truth." He gestured with the flat of his hand signifying, *Look me level in the eyes.*

"Don't use three words when one will do," he said. "Don't shift your eyes. Look always on your mark but don't stare. Be specific but not memorable, funny but don't make him laugh. He's gotta like you, then forget you the moment you've left his sight.

"And for God's sake whatever you do," he said, "don't under any circumstances—"

"Rusty, can you come here a sec?" Livingston said.

"Sure thing," Rusty said, wandering off.

Linus was left utterly bewildered, a thousand commandments to remember and fifteen minutes in which to remember them.

With twilight waning and fight time approaching, the semiindustrial section of the city out Route I-15 toward the airport was nearly deserted.

Turk and Virgil, on a tear back from the Bellagio, still in their bodyguard blazers, checked their watches as the white van careened onto a sidestreet. They were just going to make it, with no time to spare. The white van whipped around another corner and shot inside Reuben Tishkoff's warehouse, screeching to a halt near where Basher was waiting. The loading dock door closed behind them.

Inside a second van back in the shadows within the warehouse, an air freshener dangling from the rearview mirror swayed back and forth as though recently disturbed. Someone sat in the front seat of the van, in the obscurity of the shadows, watching the white van's arrival and the team members' subsequent actions.

Basher stood ready, one hand on the pinch.

Faster than a NASCAR pit crew, Basher, Turk, and Virgil loaded the pinch into the white van's rear and clambored in behind it. Turk keyed the warehouse truck door back open. Before any of them could say, "Electromagnetic pulse," the van reversed and screeched out of the warehouse fully loaded.

Left behind was the now-gutted and dismantled mock-up of the Bellagio vault, unrecognizable as such except by its makers.

Remaining behind too was the other van, whose occupant now started its engine.

The time was exactly 7:16 P.M.

The count room—behind the Bellagio's cages, where the day's gross was tallied and rectified on large tables with cameras running and a set number of observors present—was now empty.

Saul approached the central large table, hefted his briefcase onto it, and adjusted its numbered combination locks. The case opened. Inside the case, on a bed of black velvet, were five rows of glittering emeralds.

"They're very beautiful," Benedict said. "A gift?"

Lyman Zerga stared at him: his eyes told the casino magnate that it was none of his fucking business.

"Can you lift them out please?" Benedict said.

Saul lifted the velvet tray out of the case, and Benedict patted down the case's interior. Saul replaced the tray.

"All right, Mr. Zerga," Benedict said. "I acknowledge that the case does not contain any dangerous or illicit material. I further agree to take custody of your case for a twenty-four-hour period to store in our secured vault. While I cannot permit you to accompany the case to the vault—"

"Why not?" Saul demanded.

"Insurance, for one," Benedict said. "Security, another." He smiled coldly at Saul. "And I don't trust you."

There was a knock at the door, and Walsh, the casino manager, entered. A trim, understated, no-nonsense soldier, he walked around the table away from Lyman Zerga and spoke low in Benedict's ear.

"I put two plainclothes on Ocean," Walsh whispered. "He's at the keno bar now." Benedict nodded and turned his attention back to Saul.

"Mr. Zerga, this is Mr. Walsh, my casino manager," Benedict said. "If you will allow, he will arrange for your briefcase to be stored inside our vault while you watch on a security monitor.

A beat passed as the vexatious Mr. Zerga looked back and forth at the faces of Benedict and his chief lieutenant, as though trying to mind read their capacity for treachery regarding his priceless green stones.

"These are my terms," Benedict said curtly. "Yes or no?"

Saul and Benedict eyeballed each other, Saul feigning great doubt, but actually gauging how close to the other man's limit of patience to take him.

"You leave me no choice," Saul said finally. He unlocked the cuff from his wrist.

At the propped-open kitchen entrance on the alleyway behind the Bellagio, a pair of raccoons picked nearsightedly at scraps of garbage near the refuse bins.

Headlights pierced the shadows of the back alley as the white van rolled up and slowed near the entrance.

The back door to the van opened enough to unload Virgil and Turk, who had changed into waiter uniforms. They turned and pulled a table-clothed room-service cart out of the van and placed it on the pavement.

The raccoons lifted their heads, openmouthed, and sniffed the night air. Smelling trouble brewing, they lumbered off behind the bins.

Virgil and Turk hurried the cart inside, and the white van pulled away with Basher at the wheel.

*   *   *

Scoping the young man from the ground up—
the spotless pair of wingtips shifting side to side,
the hands flexing and stretching, and then the
finely tailored Saville Row threads—even his
Chicago South Side running buddies would not
have picked this guy out as Linus Caldwell.

He stood near the cage door on the north side
of the Bellagio's gaming floor, obviously waiting.
He kept an eye on the door where Benedict
would appear, and tried every trick he knew to
shake out his nerves.

From the discreet earpiece he wore, came Livingston's voice, "Deep breaths. You'll do fine."

"Thanks," Linus said as he breathed deep.

"No sweat, kid," Livingston's voice said.
"You're a rock."

Linus smiled, feeling good about himself.

"Now don't fuck up," Livingston's voice said.

Linus's smile, on Livingston's monitor up in
the Mirador Suite, disappeared as quickly as it
blossomed. Livingston watched as the team's
youngest, but hardly least important, team member continued to bounce.

Livingston's head jerked around as there was
a knock at the door.

"Room service," a voice said from the hallway.

Rusty rose from his easy chair by the window,
where he'd been enjoying a nice cigar and the
view of the sparkling, gaudy Strip. He crossed
the room and checked through the peephole,

then ushered in Turk and Virgil in waiter costumes with their room-service cart.

"Who ordered the penne?" Turk said.

Livingston raised a hand, and Turk served him his plate.

Virgil whipped off the cart's tablecloth. Underneath it was the false-lidded cash cart.

Rusty turned to the corner of the suite near the bathroom. "You ready?" he said.

Yen finished bandaging his busted hand and flexed it a few times. He nodded.

In the Bellagio "Eye in the Sky" security center, Fat and Slim sat before their monitors with their feet kicked up on the desks, watching their version of reality TV.

Behind them, Walsh, Benedict, and Saul entered.

Walsh spoke low, as though not to distract any of the operators. "This is our security center," he said to Mr. Zerga, "where we oversee all gaming in the casino as well as our vault." He pointed to the different screens. "You'll be able to monitor your briefcase from here."

Walsh, finding Fat and Slim feet up as they were, coughed.

The two watchers whipped their legs down and leapt immediately to their feet.

Benedict checked his watch.

"Don't let me keep you," Saul said.

"Mr. Zerga," Benedict said with a nod. And

much relieved finally to be free from work duties, he took his leave.

Far above in the Mirador Suite, Livingston took note and signaled Rusty.

"Linus, you're up," Rusty said into his mike.

TWENTY-FOUR

Linus, by the Bellagio cage door, nodded. He shook out his hands some more.

"Deep breaths, deep breaths," Linus said to himself.

Here came Benedict, exiting the cage, just as his assistant arrived with his portfolio—the one containing the day's new codes. The assistant made the wordless handoff and stepped aside as Benedict turned toward the restaurant where Tess was waiting for him, nursing her cocktail.

"Mr. Benedict," Linus said, stepping forward, his back held straight as he tried to look official.

"Yes?" Benedict said.

Linus presented the proper identification. "Sheldon Wills," he said. "Nevada Gaming Commission. Could I have two minutes of your time?"

Benedict sighed. He'd been sidetracked enough already this evening. "Of course," Benedict said resignedly. "Anything for the NGC."

*   *   *

At the keno bar, Danny—unaware that two plainclothes security goons watched him from across the bar—watched out of the corner of his eye as Benedict escorted Linus toward the blackjack tables. When he turned in their direction, the security detail looked away, acting invisible.

But in fact Danny wasn't turning toward them. He was watching Tess, who was rounding the corner near the restaurant, bored with waiting. Danny jumped to his feet, threw a tip on the bar, and went after her.

In the Mirador Suite, Rusty noted the time: 7:27 P.M. The time was nigh. He nodded to Yen.

Yen hopped up and tucked himself into the cash cart's hidden compartment. He prepared to fold himself down into the impossibly small space, with a slim oxygen tank for company.

Meanwhile, Rusty drilled Virgil and Turk for a final time. "Okay, when do you make the deposit?" Rusty said.

"Not until we get your signal," Turk said.

"Hey," Virgil said. "What do we look like? A couple of peckerwood jackasses or something?"

No one responded. They just looked at the two young peckerwood jackasses.

Rusty turned his attention to Yen, who took the cue and squeezed his body into the minuscule space in the cart.

"Amazing. How's it feel?" Rusty said. "You all right?"

Yen's head moved in what passed for a nod.

"What something to read?" Rusty said. "Magazine?"

From the tangle of limbs, a middle finger protruded to show Rusty what he could do with a magazine.

"Okay," Rusty said. "I'm counting down. Thirty minutes of breathing time starts . . . now."

On "now," a running clock appeared on Livingston's screen, counting down from 29:59. When it reached zero, Yen would be out of air and start to suffocate, should the operation not go as planned. The ticking-down clock would remain on Livingston's screen as a constant reminder for the duration of the first stage of the heist, the prepinch part.

Rusty sealed Yen inside the cash cart, then gave the top a tug. It was shut tight. As Virgil put the tablecloth back on the cart, Turk snatched back Livingston's penne on the way to the door and put it back on the cart with the rest of the table setting.

"You get no tip," Livingston said.

His onscreen clock read 28:37 minutes to go.

Benedict, with his codes portfolio grasped firmly in his hand, led Linus across the casino floor and up into the pit boss's station.

"It only came to our attention this morning, Mr. Benedict," Linus said. "Apparently he has a record longer than my arm."

"If he is who you say he is," Benedict said,

hailing a pit boss. "Charlie, call over Ramon Escalante."

"Certainly, Mr. Benedict," the pit boss said.

Benedict and Linus waited side by side in silence.

While Linus did his best to play it cool, Benedict dipped into his portfolio, checking to see that every item was in order.

Even as Benedict reviewed his elaborate security measures, the first attempt to steal him blind was underway, thanks to his very own need to compulsively cover every base and double-check every detail.

Far up in the Mirador Suite, Livingston had a prime overhead view of Benedict on his monitor. As the man pulled out the combination to the vault, read it, then buried it in his jacket pocket, Livingston read the material, too.

"Did you make it out?" Rusty said.

"His head blocked the last two numbers," Livingston said.

Too bad. But a foreseen contingency. On to Plan B.

"We missed it, Linus," Livingston said into his microphone. "You gotta grab the combination yourself."

25:33 minutes to go.

Linus half nodded in response, and Benedict noticed. Suspicious of the young man—as he was of everyone who represented any small deviation from routine—he decided to test him.

"You new at the commission?" Benedict said.

"Been there about two years," Linus said, glancing at Benedict as though indifferently.

"I know Hal Lindley over there," Benedict said. "You work with him at all?"

There was the slightest of pauses . . .

"Not since he died last year," Linus said, looking Benedict in the eye.

He passed.

The pit boss returned with Frank in tow.

"Mr. Escalante," Benedict said. "Would you come with us please?"

"What's this about?" Frank said.

"I think it's better if we talked off the floor," Benedict said. Linus and Benedict led Frank away.

As they passed by an elevator, its doors opened, revealing Turk and Virgil, now dressed as security guards. The two men pushed the false-lid cash cart out of the elevator ahead of them.

Had Terry Benedict been truly alert—had he not been distracted by this untimely hassle over a bad-apple employee—he might have noticed something distinctly unroutine in the elevator as he passed it. On the floor in one corner of the car were a pile of dishes, waiter uniforms, a tablecloth, and napkins left behind by the two exiting security guards.

*   *   *

Livingston and Rusty watched it all from upstairs. It was 24:26 on the clock and the clock was moving.

Pacing near the entrance to Terry Benedict's favorite restaurant was Tess, impatient at the Casino King's uncharacteristic tardiness.

A good-looking woman alone in a Las Vegas casino.

Like red meat tossed into the big-cat enclosure—sure to draw attention.

Men walking by sized her up, trying to decide if she was for sale; most of them quickly concluded that, even if so, she was well out of their range. A couple of thirty-something Alpha male wannabes veered her way, brave enough to test the market.

Tess smoothly but unmistakably shot them down by turning her back and moving toward the restaurant.

In the restaurant, a maitre d' scoured his reservations list, readying himself for the next expected customers. He peered up to find Reuben Tishkoff approaching, on either side of him two gorgeous young women, all blond hair and breasts and legs—women who wouldn't even give Hefner the time of day.

Mr. Tishkoff, of course, could not go anywhere on the Strip without being recognized. He was a longtime member of Vegas royalty, although recently deposed.

"Good evening, Mr. Tishkoff," the maitre d' said.

"Good evening, Marcel," Reuben said. "My nieces and I would like a table. Something quiet before the fight."

"I can put you at nineteen in just a couple minutes," the maitre d' said.

"Quick as you can," Reuben said, tilting his head toward the girls. "The meter's running here."

The maitre d' didn't blink an eye. He turned to his next customer. Tess was back. She, of course, merited whatever she wanted instantly.

"Miss Ocean," the maitre d' said. "Right this way . . ."

Reuben couldn't help but stare as Tess passed by. His eyes lingered a little too long and a little too low. . . .

"Hey," a voice said.

Reuben pivoted. It was Danny, and he strolled past Reuben and his lady friends and into the restaurant.

"Try to keep your tongue in your mouth," Danny said.

Reuben was shocked to see Danny—he thought he was off the job. But covering, he said, "Yeah, pal. Well only if you take your thumb out of your—"

He got jostled from behind by the two plain-clothes house goons following Danny.

"Hey! You have any idea who I think I am?" Reuben said, outraged.

* * *

Upstairs, the clock said 24:26 minutes to go.

Just as Tess was sitting down at her usual table in the restaurant, Danny approached. She went straight at him, apoplectic. "Danny, no!" she said.

"I'll just be a moment," Danny said.

"I'm having you thrown out of here," Tess said. She started past him. He grabbed her arm to keep her, and she wheeled on him.

"You're up to something, Danny," Tess said. "What? And don't say you came here for me. You're pulling a job, aren't you?"

"Tess," Danny said.

"Well, know this," she said. "No matter what it is, you won't win me back. I can't afford it."

"I just came to say good-bye," Danny said.

This surprised Tess, because something about the way he said it made her believe it. She looked at him with actual good-bye in mind, and truth be told, it saddened her. She studied him for a moment, unsure of what to say.

"Oh . . . then . . ." she said, "good-bye."

Danny started for her cheek, stopped to see if it was all right with her.

She did not recoil, but instead looked at him with something that looked a lot like regret.

He gently kissed her cheek. "Be good," he said. He turned and left her standing by the table, watching him go.

"Good-bye, Danny," Tess said, already missing

him and more than surprised at her own reaction.

Danny got as far as the restaurant's entrance, whereupon he ran smack into the plainclothes house goons.

"Mr. Ocean," the first Plainclothes Goon said. "Mr. Benedict would like to see you."

"I thought he might," Danny said with a sigh. These particular goons were much too big to tangle with.

The thugs escorted Danny away, right past Reuben and his brace of bimbos. Reuben frowned, concerned.

Eighteen and a half minutes and counting. Yen's air was nearly half gone and the operation was beginning to run a little behind schedule.

In the Bellagio casino manager's office, Ramon Escalante, the blackjack dealer—the new hire on a medical transfer from Atlantic City—stood at attention before Linus and Benedict.

Benedict checked his watch impatiently. The fight's opening bell was growing closer and closer. He was late. And he hated to be late. All the structure he'd imposed on his work life and private life was to preclude the anxiety of being late. He was fuming.

"Thank you for your cooperation, Mr. Escalante," Linus said.

Frank nodded—not at all.

"Or should I call you Mr. Catton?" Linus said.

Frank bristled, trying not to let it show. He just frowned slightly, as though puzzled.

Linus pulled out a Xeroxed mug shot and a one-page bio of Frank.

"You are Frank Catton?" he said. "Formerly of the Tropicana, the Desert Inn, and the New York State penitentiary system?"

Frank remained quiet, looking him balefully in the eye.

"Your silence suggests you don't refute that," Linus said.

"Mr. Benedict," Linus said, turning to Benedict, "I'm afraid you've been employing an ex-convict. As you know, the NGC strictly forbids—"

"Goddamn cracker," Frank said under his breath.

There was a pause. Linus turned; he couldn't believe he had just heard that. "Pardon me," he said.

"You heard me," Frank said, sneering at Linus, simmering. "Just because a black man tries to earn a decent wage in this state—"

"This has nothing to do with—" Linus said.

Frank overrode him, ranting, "—some cracker cowboy like you's gotta kick him out on the street. Want me to jump down, turn around, pick a bale of cotton! Won't let me deal cards, might as well call it whitejack."

Benedict, in a surprising display of self-control, kept his tongue and stopped himself from stomping into the middle of this; he could smell a big, fat racial-bias lawsuit brewing.

After a deep breath of disbelief, Linus said, "I resent your implication that race has anything to do with this." He turned to Benedict. "Now, as I was just saying, the Nevada Gaming Commission strictly forbids the employment of colored—" whoops, his look said—"I mean . . ."

That did it. Frank attacked Linus, lunging right at him. Linus, twisting and throwing his arms up to protect himself, contrived to dislodge the beeper from his belt. It clattered to the floor as the struggle went on.

Benedict, finally forced to act, stepped in to separate the two. As he did so, Linus deftly earned his keep. His hand dipped into Benedict's tuxedo jacket and withdrew the vault combination.

Benedict didn't have a hint of a clue. He was busy trying to keep his soon-to-be-fired employee from manhandling a member of the sacrosanct Nevada Gaming Commission.

Frank backed down from the attack after Benedict got in the middle of things. "Okay, okay, I'm cool," he said, disgusted with the lot of them.

"You all right?" Benedict said to Linus.

"Yeah," Linus said, glaring, trying to calm down. He picked up his beeper and put it on the table next to him and straightened his clothes.

*   *   *

The whole exchange fell on elated ears in the Mirador Suite. Hearing Frank's prearranged "I'm cool" line, Rusty pumped a fist. "He's got it," he said. "Virgil, Turk," he said into his mike, "deliver your package."

TWENTY-FIVE

Fourteen minutes remaining. More than half of Yen's oxygen was gone, and the enterprise was still dangerously behind schedule.

Two guards were standing sentry outside the cage door as Virgil and Turk hurried up with their cash cart. When Virgil reached for his keycard—searching for it in all his pockets—it was gone.

"Aw, Jesus," he said. "Jesus. I lost my card."

The door guards frowned at him.

A security officer approached. "What's going on here?" the security officer said.

"I think—Jesus!" Virgil said. "I lost my keycard."

This, the security officer knew, would get this guard fired. "Okay. Leave the cart," he said. "Go find it."

The security officer then turned to one of the sentries. "Take this cart inside."

The sentry nodded, swiped his keycard, and entered with the cash cart.

Turk and Virgil hesitated a moment to watch it enter, then they hurried away, Virgil still making a show of searching his pockets.

In the Bellagio "Eye in the Sky" Security Center, the monitors showed some planned and some unplanned developments, in regard to the Ocean takedown initiative.

On one monitor, the sentry pushed the Yen-filled cash cart down a cage corridor.

On another, Saul's emerald-carrying briefcase was escorted by another guard to the vault elevator.

On another, Danny was escorted inside the cage by the plainclothes goons.

"There it is now," casino manager Walsh said, referring to the arrival of the priceless briefcase at the elevator, displayed on the monitor Mr. Zerga was watching.

Saul was beginning to sweat profusely, his nerves overtaking him. He took some deep breaths and steeled himself as he watched the monitor. "Wonderful," he growled.

On the monitors, the Yen cash cart joined Saul's briefcase on the elevator.

"That's my cue," Rusty said as he exited the Mirador Suite. "Give Basher the go."

11:19 to go, Livingston's monitor showed.

"Bash, what's your status?" Livingston said into his mike.

*　　*　　*

Basher, driving the white van inside the Bellagio parking structure, was listening to a books-on-tape recording of *Jane Eyre*.

"Bash!" Livingston's voice said.

"No need to yell," Basher said, turning Brontë down.

"What's your status?" Livingston's voice said.

"I'm there," Basher said, wheeling up the last ramp. He came out into the open night air and screeched to a halt on the parking structure's top level. He looked around and saw all of Vegas in every direction.

8:36 minutes to go.

Benedict came out of the casino manager's office into the restricted interior hallway with Linus and Frank.

Benedict hailed two guards. "Please show this man off the premises." He turned to Frank. "Don't step foot in my casino again."

"Cracker," Frank said over his shoulder to Linus as he was led away.

Benedict checked his watch again. He was running really late. "Mr. Wills, if you don't mind," Benedict said.

Linus forgot to respond.

"Mr. Wills?" Benedict said.

"Of course," Linus quickly said.

They started toward the exit. But halfway there, Linus stopped.

"My beeper," he said. "I'm sorry. I forgot it."

Benedict hesitated. He was in an enormous

hurry now—he hated being behind schedule. He needed to be seen making his own grand entry into the boxing arena with Tess on his arm before the main event was called. He had to go instantly, but leaving even a member of the gaming commission alone in his cage was a security breach.

One glance at the cameras all about and he decided to risk it.

"You know how to get back out?" Benedict said.

"Of course," Linus said. "Enjoy the fight."

"Thank you," Benedict said, shaking his hand, then hurrying away.

Linus smiled after him, reaching into his pocket and fingering the page of combinations he had lifted off the man.

Yen had six minutes forty-seven seconds of oxygen left as the guards showed Frank out the front door of the Bellagio, ostensibly for the last time.

Once on the sidewalk, Frank actually tried to tip the guards. "Thanks, fellas," he said.

But the guards just growled at him and went back inside. Frank smiled and went on his way, his job complete. With luck, a dealer's job in a casino anywhere would be the last thing he would want or need in the future.

In an unmarked interrogation room somewhere back in the restricted area of the Bellagio,

Danny sat opposite the two plainclothes goons. They waited in absolute silence.

"How much longer do you think Mr. Benedict will be?" Danny said.

"Just a few minutes more," the first goon said.

Danny scanned the room. "No cameras in this room, huh?" Danny said. "Don't want anyone seeing what happens here?"

The goons said nothing. Danny checked his watch.

"He's not coming, is he?" Danny said.

The goons looked at each other; Danny had called their bluff.

"Who is?" Danny said.

There was a knock at the door, and the goons smiled.

Danny was about to find out just who was coming to join their private party.

One goon rose to usher in "the Bruiser," who had come to beat the tar out of Danny Ocean.

The Bruiser was at least six six, three hundred pounds. But it was not his size that drew attention—it was his teeth. Or the lack thereof. The Bruiser didn't hold a single incisor, molar, or bicuspid in his mouth. Gum city. There was something really terrifying about the sight.

"I guess Mr. Benedict didn't like me talking to his girl," Danny said.

The goons nodded their heads in agreement with Danny's astute assessment.

Danny smiled up at the Bruiser, and the Bruiser snarled back, showing off those gums.

He rolled up his shirtsleeves, itching to tear a hole in this man.

The goons headed for the door. "We're gonna step outside now," the first goon said. "Leave you two alone to talk things over."

The goons exited, reveling in the thought of the carnage in the offing.

The door clicked shut. Danny and the Bruiser faced off. And as Danny opened his mouth to speak, Bruiser's fist lashed out and knocked him down.

Danny rose, wiping a little blood from his lip. "Jesus, Bruiser," Danny said, "not till later."

"Sorry, Danny," the Bruiser said.

"S'okay," Danny said, shaking it off. "How's the wife?"

"Pregnant again," the Bruiser said.

"Then we'd better get to work," Danny said.

Outside the interrogation room, the goons listened with satisfaction as the sound of punches and groans floated through the door.

Inside, Danny climbed onto Bruiser's shoulders and pushed through the ceiling rafters. He took care to groan every time Bruiser slapped his fist loudly into his hand.

When a guard wheeled the cash cart with Yen and his dwindling air supply into the vault, Yen had four and half minutes of oxygen left. The guard parked the cart in a station next to its twin.

Then as an afterthought, he planted Saul's

briefcase right on top of it—*clunk*—an unfore-
seen obstacle to Yen's escape.

The guard beat a retreat from the claustropho-
bic vault.

The briefcase was registered with dismay in
the Mirador Suite. "Oh shit," Livingston said.

Saul, in the Bellagio Security Center, witnessed
the same development with the case and the
cart. He stifled a reaction.

"Does that satisfy you, Mr. Zerga?" Walsh
said.

"Yes, I'm very satisfied," Saul said.

"Close it up," Walsh said to Slim.

Slim relayed the command.

On the monitor, the vault door closed, but Saul
looked anything but satisfied. He was sweaty,
his mouth was so dry he couldn't swallow, and
he kept patting down his pockets for his Rolaids,
not finding them.

"You all right, sir?" Fat said, more concerned
than suspicious at the way Zerga's face had suddenly turned white.

In an interior hallway a level below the Security Center, Linus found his way unerringly.
Moving with circumspection, he approached the
vault-elevator door, checking up and down hallways for guards.

In his earpiece came the message from the Mirador Suite as they watched him come into view

on their monitor. "Almost there, kid," Livingston said.

At the same moment, Saul, in the Bellagio Security Center, spotted him too; and so did Fat.

"Who's that?" Fat said.

Saul could no longer handle the anxiety. His system went into overload. He gripped Fat's arm and groaned deeply. This was no ulcer problem; this was a full-fledged cardiac arrest. He slumped.

Saul passed out. "Call for a doctor," Walsh said as Walsh, Fat, and Slim all attended to him, their backs turned to the monitors.

The timing couldn't have been better. The view on one monitor displayed Linus hurrying to the elevator and punching Benedict's combination into a keypad. The elevator doors swished open for him.

Upstairs, as though he did this every night with the same precision, Livingston punched a few keys, saying, "Going to video now."

Downstairs in the security center, with Saul and his heart attack holding everyone's attention, a security monitor flipped from a shot of Linus entering the elevator to a Livingston-fed videotape of an empty lift. The elevator would stay empty as long as the tape played.

Once in the actual elevator, Linus immediately reached up to the car's ceiling and ripped down its light panel to reveal a trap door. As he started to push it open, a hand yanked it free from above, and Linus flinched back in surprise.

It was Danny.

"You didn't really think I was gonna sit this one out, did you?" Danny said with a grin.

"What? Didn't you trust me?" Linus said.

"I do now," Danny said.

He reached down and pulled Linus, wide-eyed, up to the roof of the elevator.

Three minutes of oxygen remained for Yen in the vault below.

TWENTY-SIX

The MGM Grand Garden Arena was packed with a New York/Los Angeles/Las Vegas and Everywhere-Else-of-Any-Importance crowd. It was all about bloodlust, bosoms, and being seen. Rich folk, powerful folk, and their lesser invitees all congratulated themselves at high volume for being there. People who normally loathed the idea of blood sports would have killed had they not been able to get good tickets.

A roar went up as the main-event boxers came down the aisles and entered the ring. Mike Tyson and Lennox Lewis. Gladiators. Giants. A strange bay arose from the crowd's throats, as though two primordial, larger-than-life surrogate figures were striding into the arena on their behalf—as though gods had come down to savage each other just for them.

Benedict and Tess found their ringside seats with about two minutes to spare, for the proper greetings and adulation.

Seated a row behind them, unnoticed, were Reuben Tishkoff and his "nieces."

"Ladies and gentlemen!" the ring announcer called out, and he began to introduce the combatants.

A physican approached the cage door in the Bellagio. He looked around, a bit confused, and spoke to the sentry on duty. "Someone called for a doctor?" he said.

Young Dr. Rusty Ryan it was, board-certified specialist in card hustling, high thievery, and ad-libbed flimflamming.

Meanwhile, Danny and Linus occupied the elevator shaft above the vault elevator. Danny stripped off his jacket and shirt to expose a rappelling line wrapped around his torso. Linus did the same.

"How'd you get here?" Linus asked as they prepared.

"Crawl space," Danny said. "And I had to give away a couple mil."

"But what about—I mean, that whole thing with Rusty."

Danny just smiled at him.

Had Linus been privy to the conversation that Danny and Rusty had on the balcony outside the Mirador Suite earlier that night, he'd have had no confusion.

After they fought over Tess and Rusty kicked Danny off the job, as Linus watched from inside, deaf to their remarks and blind to their expressions, Rusty followed Danny out onto the balcony, apparently to soften the blow a bit. In fact, the conversation went like this:

"You think the kid bought it?" Danny said.

"Hell, I think Reuben bought it, and he knew we were screwing around," Rusty said.

"You sure about this?" Rusty said.

Danny nodded. "Bobby Caldwell threw me into the pool the first time," Danny said. "Least I could do is give his kid a push."

Now on top of the elevator shaft, up to their necks in "the pool," Linus looked at Danny wryly. "Why'd you make me go through all this?" he said. "Why not just tell me?"

"Well, where's the fun in that?" Danny said, starting toward the elevator shaft ladder. "C'mon. Yen's got about three minutes of air left."

Danny lead Linus down and around the elevator and, side by side, they crawled onto the bottom of the elevator, gripping the undercarriage to keep from falling down the shaft. Linus inadvisedly looked down and saw how very high up they were. He tightened his grip and forgot about everything else but the task at hand: not falling.

Dr. Rusty Ryan was ushered into the Bellagio Security Center, where Lyman Zerga, aka Saul Bloom, lay unmoving on the floor.

Rusty, playing doctor, performed CPR on Saul.

Real CPR—chest pumping, listening with his stethoscope. But no mouth to mouth. At the same time, he eyeballed one of the monitors: the vault door closing, the Yen-inhabited cash cart and Saul's briefcase inside.

Rusty stopped, listened to Saul's chest again, then dropped his head. "He's gone," Rusty said.

Walsh, Fat, and Slim all bowed or shook their heads in sympathy. At the door, two paramedics arrived with a stretcher.

"You're too late, guys," Walsh said quietly. "He's dead."

The first paramedic turned to his partner. "I told you to hurry," Virgil said to Turk.

As Danny and Linus worked in the elevator shaft on the bottom of the elevator, affixing suction-cupped anchors to their rappelling lines, Danny worked to keep the kid loose.

"Who do you like tonight?" Danny said.

"Huh?" Linus said.

"Tyson or Lewis," Danny said.

"The fight . . . ?" Linus said incredulously.

Danny nodded.

"Lewis," Linus said.

Danny shot him a look.

"You like Tyson?" Linus said.

Danny nodded.

"How strongly do you feel about it?" Linus said, his genetic hustler heritage kicking in.

"You looking for action?" Danny said.

Linus shrugged.

"I'll go in for a buck," Linus said.

"A buck it is," Danny said.

They were ready, poised at the top, looking into the abyss of an elevator shaft scattered with infrared sensors—electronic daggers poised to end their grand endeavor.

"Livingston, we're set," Danny said into his mike.

Dr. Rusty led the "paramedics" out of the Bellagio cage and onto the casino floor, with "dead" Lyman Zerga on their gurney.

Lowering his head as he adjusted the blanket covering the unfortunate deceased soul, Rusty said, low, into his mike, "Livingston, we're set."

In the Mirador Suite, the numbers in the corner of Livingston's monitor said that suffocation time was upon them: twenty-one seconds of oxygen remaining.

Hearing Danny's cue, then Rusty's, Livingston said into his mike, "Basher, we're set."

Basher, fixing the pinch atop his van on the Bellagio parking lot roof, grumbled, "Just give me a minute."

"We don't have a minute," Livingston said. "Yen's gonna pass out in thirteen seconds."

"Then give me thirteen seconds," Basher said.

Basher leapt down to hook up the pinch's wires to the van's engine.

* * *

The spectacle consuming the interest of everyone else in town was reaching a fevered pitch. The crowd at the MGM Grand Garden Arena roared as the opening bell clanged for round one.

The fighters broke from their corners, menacing as assassins, as devoted to their task as executioners. They came out feinting, jabbing, moving, looking for the gap in the defenses, the chink into which to slip the stilleto.

Sitting in the first circle, ringside, practically close enough to smell the behemoths' sweat, Benedict looked at Tess, his juices flowing. He smiled as she winced at the first sharp blow.

Peering down into blackness, Danny and Linus prepared to let go at any moment.

"You ever rappelled before?" Linus said.

"Never," Danny said. "You?"

"Nope," Linus said.

How hard could it be?

Finally finished with his preparation of the pinch, Basher crouched in the van atop the Bellagio parking lot and positioned his hands on the triggering device.

"Ready," he said into his mike.

"Then hit it," Livingston's anxious voice came over his earpiece.

Basher flipped the switch.

A quick tremor, then stillness.

Basher looked out, picking a point on the horizon, like Babe Ruth, and started his count:

"One . . ." Basher said.

Distant sectors of Las Vegas began to go black, disappear from view.

"Two . . ."

Whole blocks of lights snapped off in a rapid progression inward.

By Basher's count of . . .

"Three . . ."

. . . casinos on the Strip started vanishing one by one. Every pink light of The Flamingo vanished. And then the Bellagio itself. The towering fountain in the fronting artificial lake went flaccid, sinking down to a piddle.

"Four . . ." Basher said.

At New York, New York, the giant roller coaster stopped dead; its passengers kept their arms raised, not sure what to do.

And at the MGM Grand, in the Garden Arena, where the Fracas in Vegas was in full roar, both fighters moved in simultaneously, sweat flying, both seeing an opening, gathering maximum power and firing huge lights-out overhands to the other guy's head, when every light in the arena went out.

"Four . . . Five . . ." Basher said from his rooftop aerie. The key moment was now: the point of the whole exercise with the pinch and its powerful electromagnetic pulse. Great effort for three seconds of nullity, three make-or-break seconds.

Far below, inside the underground vault elevator shaft, Danny and Linus watched as—*blip*—out went the infrared sensors, out went the crimson sabers slicing the length of the shaft into an impassable maze.

Suddenly the shaft was clear.

"Now!" Danny said.

He and Linus leaned forward and fell, their hearts in their throats, more hoping than trusting, into the darkness.

They hurtled down the elevator shaft upside down, heads curled, hearing nothing but the whoosh of their own bodies in motion and the whirl of their cords uncoiling.

"Six . . . Seven . . ." Basher counted into his headphone.

Blessedly blinded by the darkness, Danny and Linus did not have to witness the ground rising up fast to meet them, a flat slab of gray concrete—fifty feet, forty feet, thirty feet, twenty . . .

"Eight . . . Nine . . ." Basher intoned.

And—*snap*—the bungee cords reached their full extension, and Danny and Linus bounced up, the floor receding.

"Aaaaahhhhh!" Linus blurted out inadvertantly.

*   *   *

Above on the parking lot roof, Basher got
to . . .

"Ten . . ."

He whipped his head up and looked out at the
horizon again. On cue, in the distance, lights
came up. Far neighborhoods, nearer ones, then
the Strip too. First the lights at the Mirage began
flashing back on, then at the MGM, fast approaching the Bellagio.

As he and Linus came to a near standstill in
midair about ten feet above the concrete floor,
Danny quickly withdrew a slim blade, grabbed
the two cords and slashed them straight across.
He and Linus went tumbling to the floor, and all
importantly, their drop lines recoiled lightning
fast back up the long shaft to their elevator anchors, just milliseconds before the infrared lights
went back on-line.

In the prizefight arena at the MGM Grand, the
lights suddenly flashed back on, revealing both
fighters standing, disoriented. Tyson recovered
first, and capitalized on Lewis's disorientation
by throwing a sucker punch to his jaw.

And literally before the crowd knew what
happened, down went Lewis, and Tyson backed
away.

A stark, momentary lull, then up went the
crowd, roaring. . . .

"One . . . two . . . three . . ." the ref barked, beginning his count.

Benedict, up on his feet, watched in horror as the count went to ten and the fight was over. He made a quick visual survey. The arena was apoplectic over the bizarre blackout/knockout.

"What the hell was that?" Benedict said.

He craned his neck, looking rapidly around the room, surveying his empire. He smelled a rat. His eyes fell on Reuben behind him.

But Reuben just shrugged, equally mystified: I didn't pull the plug.

"The first goddamn round," Benedict said in disgust.

Basher looked out on Las Vegas from a far different perspective. From where he stood on the roof, the tiny hiccup in the torrent of power that gushed so steadily from the Colorado River through Las Vegas was a moment of perfection, a masterwork of performance art. It was a never-to-be-repeated but, he hoped, forever-to-be-celebrated thing of beauty.

Basher observed his achievement with great pride, his job complete. "Viva Las Vegas," he said.

TWENTY-SEVEN

Linus and Danny got up from where they'd landed on the elevator shaft floor, clutching their heads and rubbing bruises. Linus shook off the fall, but Danny didn't recover so quickly.

"You all right?" Linus said.

"No, but you're sweet to ask," Danny said.

A dozen paces away, inside the Bellagio vault, the lights were just flickering on. At that moment, the false lid of the cash cart thrust upward slightly—funambulist Yen was out of air and he was trying to get out . . .

Only at that instant was Yen becoming aware of something heavy resting atop the cash cart lid. Saul's emerald case.

Livingston caught sight of the moving lid with the attaché case just as his own monitors came flickering back on. The video master had his fingers poised on a PLAY button, ready to initiate the next phase of programmed deception, as Frank came in the door.

"Are they in?" Frank said.

"One second," Livingston said. He looked up at Frank and did a double take.

"I thought you got kicked out?" he said.

Frank shrugged.

Abruptly one of Livingston's monitors—monitor A—aligned itself. The view was an overhead security-cam view of the vault corridor, where three guards with Uzis stood idly, on duty. A second window on the monitor showed the interior of the vault itself: the cash cart lid moving and Yen trying to get out.

Livingston pressed PLAY.

On monitor B, the same scene flashed but with a difference. Same overhead security-cam view of the vault corridor; same three Uzi guards standing idly, on duty . . . but in totally different positions. And in the window showing the vault: two cash carts, but no Zerga briefcase, no Yen.

"This tape's from last night," Livingston explained. "Same guards, same"—his eyes fixed on Saul's briefcase pushing closer to the edge of the cash cart, dangerously close to crashing to the floor, as Yen tried to free himself—"shift," Livingston went on distractedly, his mind on the mini drama on screen.

In the Bellagio "Eye in the Sky" Security Center, the banks of monitors came back on when Livingston's did, and for a beat, the vault moni-

tor showed the cash cart lid moving strangely—
but then it switched abruptly to the placid image
from Livingston's monitor B.

As the team had calculated, at the moment
Livingston activated the tape on Monitor B,
switching to the bogus vault feed the Bellagio
watchers would see, the "Eye in the Sky" was
seething with confused activity. When their
monitors flickered back on, every watcher in the
place glommed on to a floor monitor, watching
the gambling tables.

Predictably, the floor was going nuts. After the
ten seconds of darkness, all bets were off. Ten
seconds of pitch-blackness in a casino meant free
money. Some players had doubled-down during
the blackout. Others had miraculously halved
their bets. Dozens of gamblers had transparent
Who me? looks on their faces, while others sat
there wearing their best poker faces.

Livingston's video feed switch went unnoticed. Leaving the field clear for Danny and
Linus to pry open the elevator doors and
squeeze out into the first hallway unseen.

Just beyond the next doorway stood the three
Uzi-carrying, night-shift guards, hovering outside the vault door, wondering what the hell just
happened to the lights.

On the other side of the vault door, Yen continued to push up on the cash cart lid. The more he
pushed, the more Saul's briefcase slid off. Yen,
realizing by now what it was, stretched his hand
out to grab it. But the case had slid beyond his

reach, to the edge of falling on the sensor-laden floor of the vault, threatening to blow the whole brilliant heist sky-high right then and there.

In the corridor, the Uzi guards shifted around, talking, speculating about the short blackout. When all their backs were turned to the elevator shaft, Linus and Danny appeared briefly in the doorway. They snapped gas pellets and slid them into the corridor.

The first Uzi-carrying guard sniffed something. "Jesus, Ron, was that you?" he said.

Linus and Danny waited, Danny silently mouthing a three count, until . . .

Thud . . .

Thud . . . thud . . .

They peered around the corner to see all three Uzi-carrying guards lying unconscious on the ground. Linus started in, but Danny held him back. "Not yet," Danny said.

A beat passed; another beat, then: "Okay," Danny said.

Danny and Linus entered the vault corridor, waving the faint remnants of the gas away from their faces, tiptoeing past the guards' bodies.

"You think Yen made it out okay?" Linus said.

"I'm sure he's fine," Danny said.

Yen's supple arm stretched farther out of the cash cart, twisting around, trying for an angle that would facilitate a grab. He pushed up just a little more on the false lid, pushed his arm out a little farther, until the briefcase broke loose, and tumbled sickeningly toward the floor.

But Yen's incredibly quick arm and hand snaked out and snagged the handcuff chain attached to the case and swung it round. It came within millimeters of touching the floor. But just missed.

He'd got it.

That threat over, Yen threw open the cash cart lid, sat up, and gulped down the biggest breath of air in his life.

Out in the vault corridor, Linus extracted from his pocket the fruits of his Nevada Gaming Commission masquerade: the day's new codes. He punched in the code for the door to the vault anteroom. He stepped back, waiting. It slid open, revealing the vault door. It was sleek, immense, and impregnable.

"Jesus," Linus said, his jaw dropping.

"There's a Chinese man with a hundred sixty million dollars behind that door," Danny said. "Let's get him out." Danny took a flat hand and slapped the door hard.

Yen waited inside the vault, perched atop the cash cart, with Saul's briefcase opened beside him, Lyman's "emeralds" lying exposed. He heard Danny's muffled slaps and he knew it was time for his leap. It was the exact same distance as the leap he had made in the practice session, but this time he only had one good hand.

*   *   *

Whistling past the graveyard, Frank—upstairs in the Mirador Suite—tried the reverse jinx. "Fin says he shorts it," Frank said.

"No bet," Livingston said. Too incredibly much at stake.

Yen prepared for his leap, then sprung across the room, to the ledge he had to grab. And he grabbed it desperately with his only good hand. He felt himself slipping right away, and in a second he would hit the sensored floor. In a flash, he spun and split his legs, propping himself up between two adjoining walls, inches above the floor. An acrobatic wonder.

Frank and Livingston, watching the monitor, exhaled.

"Shit," Livingston said, now wishing he had bet.

Outside the vault, Danny, oblivious to the close call, slapped the door again. A moment passed. Then Yen responded with a slap of his own on the door.

"Okay," Danny said.

Basher joined Livingston and Frank at the monitor upstairs, as Linus punched in another combination he stole from Benedict. At the same time, Danny unraveled a thin electrical wire connected to a detonator.

"That's it?" Frank said.

"There's still the five pins and the floor sensor," Livingston said. "Not much we can do about that from this side of the door. But from this side . . ."

He punched up the image of Yen in the vault.

"A little bit of Semtex should do the trick," Basher said.

They watched as Yen set the last of Lyman Zerga's "emeralds" in place against the vault door. He affixed a detonator receiver about the size of a golf pencil to the string of plastic explosive, then slapped the door twice.

Outside the vault, Danny responded with two slaps of his own. He stepped back, detonator in hand, its wire attached to the vault door. "Counting down from twenty," Danny said, checking his watch. "Now."

Yen started his retreat from the vault door, but got yanked back. His hand's bandage was caught on the door.

On the other side of the vault door, Danny counted, "Seventeen, sixteen, fifteen. . . ."

Yen feverishly tried to free himself, but he couldn't use his other hand lest he drop to the floor. He tried gnawing at his bandage, which brought his face within inches of a plastic explosive.

"Eleven, ten, nine. . . ." Danny counted.

Livingston and company, alert to Yen's lethal predicament, reacted. "Linus, can you read me?"

Livingston said into his mike. "Linus, do not blow the door. You're about to kill Yen."

At the vault door, Linus heard nothing through his earpiece.

"Five, four, three . . ." Danny said.

Inside, Yen finally freed himself.

But at the same instant on the other side of the door, Danny said, "One," and pressed his detonator. . . .

TWENTY-EIGHT

Inside the vault, nothing happened. No explosion.

Yen, still on the door, remained frozen. Trembling.

A beat.

Still nothing.

Yen began to creep back, leaping onto a money shelf, then another, as far from the explosives as he could get.

Outside the vault, Danny pressed the detonator again. Still nothing.

"What's wrong?" Linus said.

"I don't know," Danny said.

Linus came over to look. "You check the batteries?" he said.

Danny blanched.

Linus shot him a look. *Are you kidding me?*

Livingston, Frank, and Basher watched this development on the Mirador Suite monitors.

Their hearts fell. They looked at each other in disbelief.

Saul entered, back from death by cardiac arrest and dressed as himself again. His job was complete.

"Everything going okay?" he said.

Danny checked his batteries. He had the types with the little built-in power test strips: both read 0%.

Linus turned, looked down at the unconscious Uzi-carrying guards. He lunged for their gear, ransacking it for replacements. He found AA's in their flashlights.

"You know, you lose focus for one second in this game—" Linus said.

"And someone gets hurt, yeah yeah," Danny said. "I don't hear Yen complaining."

He took the batteries, inserted them in his detonator, then slapped the door twice more.

Inside, Yen caught his breath on the far end of the room. He heard the slap, rolled his eyes, and ducked out of the line of fire.

Danny pressed the detonator.

On the inside of the vault door, the Semtex emeralds exploded.

Danny and Linus heard several muted but powerful blasts.

Linus inched forward, almost dreading this moment. He paused.

"Do it," Danny said.

Linus pulled . . . and the door opened.

Danny and Linus touched fists in the briefest of celebrations and entered the vault.

Silence.

The cash carts had crumpled, and the vault gratings, blackened, had held.

"Amazing?" Danny said.

Linus went to one of the racks and tentatively opened it.

Yen popped up from within. With his hair on end, he looked as if he'd just dropped out of a cyclone.

"Where the fuck you been?" Yen said, finally using English.

Livingston, Frank, Saul, and Basher watched the monitor as the first wave of cash packets got tossed onto the vault floor.

"Ever been in love?" Saul said.

"No, I guess not," Frank said, considering it for a moment. "Not really."

"This is better," Saul said.

The guys turned to look at him and smiled.

Saul smiled back for the first time since the whole operation began. Things were finally unfolding exactly according to plan.

"Rusty, you're up," Livingston said into his mike.

Outside the fight arena at the MGM Grand, Rusty pushed back into the exit as people streamed past him on their way out. He moved to a spot to one side of the traffic flow and dialed his cell phone. He listened.

Below, in the arena, Benedict and Tess were pushing their way out through the crowd. A phone began ringing nearby . . . again and again.

"You gonna answer it?" Benedict said.

"I don't have a cell phone," Tess said.

They kept moving, but the ring pursued them. Finally, Benedict stopped, pulled Tess's purse from her shoulder and opened it: inside, he found a cell phone, ringing.

"It isn't mine," Tess said, bewildered.

"See who's on the other end," Benedict said.

She took the phone and activated it.

"Hello?" Tess said.

"May I have a word with Mr. Benedict please?" Rusty said.

Tess looked up, confused. "It's for you," Tess said.

Benedict took the phone. "Who the hell is this?" Benedict said.

Rusty, in the distance, at the arena's exit, out of sight of either Benedict or Tess, spoke into the phone. "The man who's robbing you," he said.

TWENTY-NINE

Benedict strode into the Bellagio Security Center nearly out of control with rage and unaccustomed fear.

Tess walked in with him, nursing a bad feeling of her own.

The Eye in the Sky buzzed with normal activity, by all appearances.

Benedict kept the cell phone pressed to his ear, while he barked at Fat, "What the hell is going on down there in the vault?"

"Nothing, sir," Fat said. "All normal."

"Show me," Benedict said.

Fat pointed to the security-cam view of the vault corridor and the vault—Livingston's tape.

"All quiet," Fat said.

"I'm afraid you're mistaken," Benedict said into the phone venomously.

Benedict's voice came out over a small speaker in the Mirador Suite. Frank, Basher, and Saul listened and watched the monitors over Livingston's shoulder as the phone conversation ensued.

"You're watching your monitor?" Rusty's voice said. "Okay, keep watching."

Livingston punched in some numbers on a keypad in front of him.

In the Eye in the Sky, Fat's monitor flickered and new images suddenly appeared.

Three masked men in the impregnable Bellagio vault threw stacks of money onto the floor; three Uzi guards lay bound and unconscious in the corridor.

The security center, understandably, erupted in exclamations and flurried activity.

"Jesus Christ," Benedict said.

Rusty, strolling casually through the Bellagio, was so nonchalant, there was no reason anyone passing him would have suspected he was doing more on his cell phone than ordering a pizza. "In this town," he said to Benedict, "your luck can change just that quickly."

Benedict was close to apoplectic. He took a breath and cupped the phone, then barked at Walsh: "Find out how much money we have down there," Benedict said.

Tess, amid all this chaos, was still curious. How did that cell get into her handbag? And suddenly it hit her: earlier that evening . . . in the restaurant with Danny. She replayed the moment.

"Good-bye," Danny said.

He started for her cheek, stopped to see if it was all right with her.

She, sad eyed, did not recoil.

He leaned forward and gently kissed her cheek . . . and slipped the cell phone into her handbag, unnoticed. "Be good," he said.

Tess had to stifle her shock.

"Tess," Benedict said. "Tess, perhaps you might care to . . ."

Tess snapped back and turned toward him, not sure what to say. "Perhaps I might care to what?" Tess said.

"Perhaps . . . I think it would be better if you weren't here for this," Benedict said.

"I'll see you upstairs," Tess said, not happy that she was being shooed away like a child. She started to exit, debating whether to speak up about her cell-phone realization. She turned back, ready to spill, but Benedict was too busy for her.

"All right," Benedict said on the phone. "You've proven your point. You've broken into my vault. Congratulations. You're a dead man."

Tess left.

"Maybe." Rusty's voice said.

"May I ask how do you expect to leave here, hmm?" Benedict said. "Do you believe I'll simply allow you to parade bags full of money out my casino doors?" Still, Benedict had no idea who he was talking to or where the caller was.

Rusty was no more than a few dozen yards away on Benedict's own gaming floor. A distance beyond Rusty, Tess exited the cages. She stopped, puzzling over what to do . . . and happened to spot him.

"No," Rusty said. "You're gonna carry it out for us."

Benedict had to laugh. "And why would I do that?" Benedict said.

"Take a closer look at your monitor," Rusty said.

Benedict stared at the vault monitor. The three masked men stuffed money into large canvas bags and marked the bags with X's. They were leaving another portion of cash untouched, but clearly rigged with a bomblike device: booby-trapped.

"As your manager's probably reporting to you by now," Rusty's voice said, "you have a little over a hundred sixty million in your vault tonight."

And as if Rusty were in the room watching, Walsh approached with the night's cash count, written on a piece of paper: $163,156,759.

"You may notice we're only packing up about half," Rusty said. "The other half we're leaving in your vault, booby-trapped, as a hostage."

Rusty continued to walk the crowded casino floor, talking quietly on his cell. "You let our eighty million go, and you get to keep your eighty," Rusty said. "That's the deal. You try and stop us, we'll blow both cash loads."

Rusty heard something behind him. He spun around—and came face-to-face with Tess.

She stared at him directly. She knew.

Rusty held her glance. "Mr. Benedict, you can lose eighty million dollars secretly tonight or you can lose a hundred and sixty million dollars publicly," Rusty said. "It's your decision." He cupped the phone.

"Hi," Rusty said to Tess.

Benedict got the picture. He was nothing if not a quick study. These goniffs, whoever they were, had set it up to try to make him play accomplice in his own ruin. He cupped his phone too and vented his rage. He knew what he should do— let the money go. And he knew what he wanted to do—stop these sons of bitches at all costs.

He made his choice. "Make the call," Benedict said to Walsh.

Walsh grabbed a phone, punched numbers.

"911," a voice said. "Emergency response."

Thanks to his hear-all, see-all, tell-all "spider," Livingston was listening right in on the call.

"Hello, this is Mr. Walsh at the Bellagio," Walsh's voice said. "We have an incident here."

"Okay," Benedict said to Rusty, uncupping his phone. "You have a deal."

* * *

Tess and Rusty held a stare as Rusty held the phone, covered.

"Where's Danny?" Tess said.

"He's fine," Rusty said. "He wants you to go upstairs and watch TV."

Tess was a little pissed at all the dismissal. "He does?" Tess said.

"You have a deal," Benedict's voice repeated on the phone.

"It's all right, Tess," Rusty said away from the covered mouthpiece. "I promise."

Then back into the phone, he said, "Good. Here's what you do. Five minutes from now, the men in the vault are going to deposit six bags in the vault elevator."

Tess wasn't sure what to do. As Rusty continued on the phone, she backed off, debating if she could really blow the whistle on her ex.

Below ground, six canvas bags—each sealed tight, each marked with an X—were being loaded onto the vault elevator.

"If they meet anyone," Rusty's voice said in Benedict's ear, "we'll blow the money in the bags and the money in the vault." A pause for emphasis. "One minute after that," Rusty continued, "the elevator will rise to your cages."

Benedict watched on his monitor as a small cadre of guards awaited the arrival of the vault elevator. Its doors opened to reveal the six large canvas bags, each sealed tight, marked with an X.

Rusty's voice said, "Six of your guards will pick up the bags and carry them out into the casino."

Six guards did precisely that.

"If they take more than twenty seconds to reach the casino floor," said Rusty as he moved past the slot machines, "or if there's any indication a switch has been made, we'll blow the money in the vault and the money in the bags."

A slot machine suddenly rang behind him, announcing a jackpot payoff.

Benedict heard the slot machine. "He's in the casino right now," Benedict said to Walsh.

"Of course I'm in the casino," Rusty's voice said. "In fact, I'm staying in your hotel. And I have two words for you: mini bar." Then, turning back to business, Rusty continued: "Now, as soon as your guards hit the casino floor . . ."

The six guards carrying the six X-marked bags appeared from the cage door. . . .

". . . an unmarked white van is going to pull up in your valet station," Rusty said.

The six guards, escorted by Bellagio security, carried the money bags out of the building.

The white van, now clean of the NEVADA TELE-COM sign, idled before the Bellagio, its windows tinted, the driver's identity inscrutable. It was swarmed by security, but they maintained a wide perimeter.

"Your guards will load the bags into the van's rear," Rusty's voice said. "If anyone so much as approaches the driver's door, we blow everything."

The guards complied, and carried out the money and loaded it into the van's rear. There, they found a video camera mounted on the backseat of the van monitoring them. They still could not catch a glimpse of the driver. They closed the van doors.

The white van departed the Bellagio valet station, clandestinely shadowed by five sedans—sedans riding low, heavily laden with Benedict's security goons.

Meanwhile, behind the casino, a SWAT van arrived and unloaded its squad.

"Now what?" Benedict said into his cell.

"Now," Rusty's voice said, "when I get word that the van hasn't been followed, that the money is secure, my men will exit the building, and once their safety is confirmed, you'll get your vault back."

In the Bellagio Security Center, Walsh mouthed to Benedict, "Swat team is here."

Benedict nodded and threw him a thumbs-up.

"Sir, I have complied with your every request—would you agree?" Benedict said.

"I would," Rusty's voice said.

"Good," Benedict said. "Now I have one of my own."

"Yes?" Rusty's voice said.

"Run and hide," Benedict said, at last able to release his venom. "If you get picked up next week buying a hundred-thousand-dollar sports car in Newport Beach, I'll be supremely disappointed. Because I want my people to find you. And rest assured when they do, they won't hand you over to the police."

Malignant silence.

"Run and hide," Benedict said. "That's all I ask."

Above, in the Mirador Suite, Livingston's monitors still displayed the masked men in the vault, as well as the elevator and its shaft, and the cage and its corridors. But the suite itself was empty.

THIRTY

The white van navigated the Las Vegas Strip, taking care to observe all traffic laws, and turned off on the road to the airport.

The five sedans tailed the van tightly, security goons in each checking their weapons and confering about the choice of incendiaries and concussion explosives they would use to take the robbers out.

Unnoticed, not far behind the cavalcade, was a familiar Rolls Royce, tailing them.

Tess, pacing in Benedict's suite, bit her nails, debating whether to call the police right away and turn in Danny.

A local TV newscast buzzed with the contentious aftermath of the prizefight. It meant nothing to Tess. She didn't even hear it, so consumed was she with the decision she had to make, the hardest of choices. She knew exactly what she should do, what any rational person would do. . . .

* * *

On Benedict's monitor, the Uzi guards, bound and unarmed on the floor outside the Bellagio vault, remained unconscious to the activity within the vault. He listened to the phone line to the robber—it had gone dead.

Rusty's cell phone now lay open and un-manned on a corner of the railing around the slot-machine bay.

Benedict hung up.

"Our guys say the van is headed toward Mc-Carran Airport," Walsh said.

"Get everyone in position," Benedict said. "I want my vault back before that van hits the tar-mac."

The SWAT team, six men in all, hustled through the cage corridors armed to the teeth, with body armor and helmets and vision guards. They were as faceless as storm troopers. Regular staffers stayed out of the way of their bristling weaponry.

The white van convoy approached McCarran Airport, driving at a very deliberate speed. They were shadowed still by the Rolls Royce—which might as well have been invisible, so intent were the goons on the white van.

* * *

Benedict scanned the monitors showing his vault, where the three masked men paced beside the booby-trapped money. He studied the men: they gave away nothing as far as their identity was concerned. They were too well covered.

Abruptly Benedict said, "Where's Zerga?" He was not in the Security Center where Benedict had left him.

No immediate answer came.

"Mr. Zerga?" Benedict repeated when he saw Walsh's sheepish look. "With the briefcase?"

"He's—he died," Walsh said.

Benedict shot him a slow, sideways glance.

The SWAT team, now ready, rappelled down the elevator shaft—a shaft whose infrared sensors had been turned off by Walsh. The commandos moved into position.

The "Eye in the Sky" monitors showed their position.

"Night goggles on," the SWAT leader's voice said over the radio. "Prepare to cut power."

Fat removed the safety lock and readied the power switch. "Ready when you are," he said.

Benedict scoured the monitors. The masked men continued to pace on one screen. The SWAT team prepared to invade on another. "Do it," Benedict said.

"Cut it," the SWAT leader said over the radio.

Fat flipped the power switch.

*   *   *

Finally, in the Mirador Suite, all of Livingston's monitors went black.

The many monitors in the Bellagio Security Center went black as well, but Benedict still had ears. He listened closely to the SWAT frequency.

"First wave in!" the leader's voice said over the SWAT frequency. "Second wave, now!" Then there was running, panting, then Linus's voice, distant and panicked.

"Guys, someone's here!" Linus's voice said.

"Take him down! Now!" the leader's voice said.

A brief spurt of automatic weapons fire . . . BARRROOOOM!

Dead silence descended over the Eye-in-the-Sky. Slim stared deep into a monitor's dark pitch.

"Lights!" The leader's voice said over the SWAT frequency. "We need power now!"

Fat flipped the power back on.

And on the monitors, visions of destruction down below materialized. Smoke filled the vault as two SWAT members pushed through it. Other SWAT members helped evacuate the unconscious guards.

"What's the situation down there?" Benedict said into an intercom.

"They blew it," the SWAT leader's voice said. "They blew the . . . oh Jesus . . . if there was anyone in there, they're not in one piece anymore."

Benedict spun and barked to Walsh: "Tell

them to take the van." Then he said soberly, "I'm going down there."

As an afterthought, he said to Slim, "Find out how they fiddled with our cameras."

The white van, along with its tailing caravan, made the loop at McCarran Airport, and then took the charter service turnoff, pulling in at one of the dozen charter airlines entrances. It crossed into the parking area and stopped.

The five sedans converged on the van, tires screeching, lurching to a stop. Goons in multiples of four and five emerged, locked and loaded.

"Get out of the van! Now!" screamed a goon armed with an automatic assault rifle.

No response came from within the van. The head goon signaled. The others responded, raising their weapons and shooting the van's tires flat.

Slim, as directed, was trying to find out what the hell the thieves had done to the house communications setup. He nosed around the wiring in the circuitry room. Reaching deep into a mesh, he found a foreign object: Livingston's "spider."

He yanked it out.

Below ground, the vault elevator doors opened and Benedict made his way into the smokey corridor. He passed the Uzi guards, awake now and stumbling along, being helped by the SWAT team members to the elevator.

Benedict arrived at the door to his demolished vault. Everything within—the money, Lyman Zerga's emeralds, and people as well—had to have been destroyed.

"Mr. Benedict," said the approaching SWAT team leader.

"Yes," Benedict managed.

"We couldn't find any survivors," he said. "Or, I'm afraid, any of your money. I'm sorry, sir."

Benedict didn't want to hear any more. They had all failed him. "Take your men out," he said.

The SWAT team leader stepped away and barked at his men, "Okay, guys, grab your gear and clear out."

As they hurriedly did so, Benedict, seething, spoke into his walkie-talkie. "Walsh, how are we with the van?"

At McCarran Airport, the stalemate with the van continued. The van just sat there, no doors opening, no sign of movement from inside.

"Out of the van now!" the head goon said. "Hands up!"

An employee from the charter airline stuck his head out of his office door into the night. "Hey, what's going on here?" the employee said innocently.

A half dozen firearms turned and pointed in

his direction. The employee disappeared back inside his office at once.

The head goon cautiously approached the van, reached for the driver's door, and yanked it open.

As he ducked back, the rest could see into the cab. There was no driver.

Where there should have been a driver, there was a videocamera mounted at eye level.

The head goon craned back his head, looking the van over, completely befuddled. Only then did he notice, for the first time, an enormous antenna sprouting from the van's rear bumper.

The van suddenly lurched.

A distance away, on line of sight but inconspicuously positioned, was the Rolls Royce.

Inside the Rolls, seated next to Reuben Tishkoff, was Virgil Malloy. In his hands was a remote control, complete with a tiny video monitor displaying the van driver's point of view. It had a steering mechanism, and it was a near-replica of the one Virgil used in the monster-truck drag race against his brother back in Utah.

Virgil used it now as he watched the goons scramble back from the lurching flat-tired van.

"Enough monkey business," Reuben said.

Virgil brought the van to a stop, then primed a distinctive red button on his remote.

As the head goon reached for the rear door, his hand inches away . . .

BARRROOOOM!

The door exploded open and, knocked on his

ass, the head goon watched as the canvas X bags within burned to cinders.

The goons stood there stupidly, watching the flames.

Then the head goon noticed something of interest. One burning shred of paper dislodged from a bag. It wasn't burning money. It was a promotional flier for a call-girl service.

THIRTY-ONE

Benedict stepped over the scattered remains of his vault. He picked up a fragment of a cash cart, burned to a crisp, and let it drop.

"Mr. Benedict," Walsh's voice said over the walkie-talkie.

"Yes?" Benedict said.

"They took the van," Walsh's voice said.

"And?" Benedict said.

"And they blew up the bags, sir," Walsh's voice said hesitantly. This was bad news.

Benedict dropped his walkie-talkie to his side. "Shit," he said.

"Sir . . . Sir . . ." Walsh's voice said. He didn't know if the rest he had to tell was good news or bad.

"What, Walsh?" Benedict said.

"They say it doesn't look like there was any money in the bags, sir," Walsh's voice said.

"What?" Benedict said.

"They say the bags were filled with fliers," Walsh said. "For hookers."

"What do you mean there was no money in the bags?" Benedict said.

"That's what they said, sir," Walsh's voice said. "I don't understand it. We both saw them putting money inside those bags."

Benedict stopped cold. He stared up at a wall, where a hanging engraved sign reading BELLAGIO had been smoke-stained.

"Walsh, cue up the tape of the robbery," Benedict said immediately.

Walsh stood before several monitors in the Bellagio Security Center as Slim cued up the masked men robbing the vault a few minutes ago, displaying it beside the present image of Benedict staring at the vault wall.

"Does it say Bellagio on the south wall of the vault?

In the image with the masked men going about their looting, it did not, in fact, say Bellagio on the vault's south wall.

"No, sir," Walsh said on the walkie-talkie. "I—I don't understand. . . ."

Benedict exhaled in sudden realization. "We had that sign installed on Tuesday," Benedict said. "The image we saw of the men robbing us was a tape."

"What?" Walsh's voice said.

"Someone built a double of my vault," he said, "then made a tape of them robbing it. When we saw them putting money in those bags, that wasn't actually happening."

Walsh's jaw dropped as he watched the tape again. "Then, sir . . ." he said.

Below in the ruined, desecrated vault, Benedict was absolutely fucking furious.

"What happened to all the money?" Walsh's voice said.

All the money—nearly $160,000,000 in cash— was still in the Bellagio, but only momentarily.

The SWAT leader was leading his men out through the casino and lounge. Each of them— eight men in all—carried a large SWAT duffel bag, ostensibly for all their weapons. As the eight commandos passed out of range of the casino cameras, they stripped off their riot head gear, revealing their faces for the first time.

It was Rusty, in full regalia, leading Livingston, Turk, Saul, Frank, Basher, Yen, and Linus out of the Bellagio, each dressed as a SWAT member. Each carrying a duffel bag with nearly twenty million dollars in it.

"What happened to all the money?"

It was Walsh's 160-million-dollar question.

Walsh's urgent 911 call twenty minutes earlier at the height of the heist?

Livingston took that call upstairs in the Mirador Suite, as Basher, Saul, and Frank got into SWAT gear ten feet from him.

"911," Livingston said. "Emergency response."

Had Walsh been able to watch a full array of properly working monitors and been able to see through the disguises, he would have seen exactly what happened to his money.

Turk Malloy and friends, dressed as armed SWAT team members, hustled along a cage corridor. SWAT member Saul Bloom had trouble rappelling down the shaft with the rest. SWAT commando Basher Tarr took position next to SWAT leader Rusty Ryan at the elevator shaft's bottom. A few feet away from them—off-camera—Danny Ocean sat smiling. "Prepare to cut power!" SWAT team leader Rusty Ryan shouted in his disguised voice. SWAT commando/the Amazing Yen lit a short fuse leading into the vault. Linus Caldwell, feigning hysteria, shouted, "Guys, someone's in here!" SWAT leader Rusty Ryan fired a spurt of bullets. *BARRROOOOM!*

No one was hurt.

Nor was the money hurt.

Millions in cash, stacked neatly and safely in the corridor outside the vault, sat ready to be transported.

Thieved . . .

Liberated . . .

Packed into the phony SWAT team's duffel bags and carried out right under Terry Benedict's nose.

*   *   *

The SWAT team exited the Bellagio and boarded the second vehicle Turk and Virgil had been working on all this time, the one in the warehouse with the air freshener hanging from its rearview mirror.

The one done up as an exact replica of a SWAT van.

Turk took the wheel as the others jumped in the back. Rusty stuck his head into the front compartment and said, "Hit it."

Turk hit the gas and the vehicle peeled away, carrying its cadre of new multimillionaires far away from the Bellagio.

THIRTY-TWO

Back in the Bellagio vault, Benedict squatted down to inspect a burned scrap of paper on the vault floor. It, too, was a flier for a strip joint.

And it finally occurred to him: "Ocean," Benedict said.

He was out of the vault and up in the cage in less than two minutes. Heated, obsessed, he came up fast on the interrogation room, where his plainclothes goons kept watch.

"Where's Ocean?" Benedict said.

"Still inside, sir," the first plainclothes goon said. "With Bruiser."

Benedict straightened his cuffs, cooled himself. Then he said, "Open that door."

As the door to the interrogation room swung open, it was to the sight of Bruiser throwing a mean left hook across Danny's face.

Benedict stepped in.

Bruiser saw him and stepped away, toweling off his bloodied knuckles.

Benedict stepped near and studied Danny. The man was a bloody mess, head rolling, eyes puffed up.

"Wake him up," Benedict said.

The goons stepped in, slapped Danny alert.

At last, Danny recognized Benedict in the room. "Hiya, Benedict," Danny said, a little punchy. "How's the other fight going?"

Benedict kept his cool. "Did you have a hand in this?" he said.

Danny looked at him, drifting in and out.

"Did you?" Benedict demanded.

"Did I have a hand in what?" Danny said, trying to focus.

Benedict scrutinized Danny. Was he bluffing? He looked at Bruiser, then at Danny again, and decided no.

"Get him out of here," Benedict said.

As the goons scooped him up and dragged him out, Danny caught Bruiser's eye for just a moment. And barely winked.

The phone rang upstairs in Benedict's suite.

Tess plucked it up. "Hello?" she said.

"Turn to Channel 88," a voice that could have been Dell Livingston's voice said.

Click. Tess keyed the remote and turned to Channel 88.

A security camera angle of the cage hallway

appeared on the screen. The goons appeared, escorting bloodied Danny out.

Tess gasped, frozen.

Benedict appeared, a few paces behind Danny.

Danny glanced back to see Benedict, brooding. What was his next step?

Just then, Walsh came down the hallway.

"You get robbed or something, Benedict?" Danny said thickly, through his bloodied mouth. "Geez, that's a shame."

Benedict looked up, suspicious. "Stop there," Benedict said.

The goons stopped, spun Danny around to face Benedict.

"Where. Is. My. Money," Benedict seethed.

They held each other's eye.

"What would you say," Danny said, "if I told you you could get your money back . . ."

Long pause.

Benedict waited.

". . . if you gave up Tess?"

He had Benedict's attention.

"What would you say?" Danny.

"I would say yes," Benedict said.

Tess, watching the live feed on Benedict's TV, was wild-eyed with fury.

"Well, that's very interesting . . ." Danny said. Another pause.

". . . but I didn't have anything to do with it."
He grinned.

Benedict sank. "Escort Mr. Ocean to the exit,"
he said to his goons dismissively. "And contact
the police. I would imagine Mr. Ocean is in violation of his parole."

On Benedict's TV in his suite upstairs, the picture showed the goons hauling Danny out. The
suite's door was just closing.

Tess had left, heartbeats ago.

"Maybe we should have held him," Walsh
said.

"No," Benedict said. "Follow him. Everywhere."

Benedict walked out the security door and
took in his casino. It had been a bad night. He
was down a hundred and sixty million.

With less than his usual Master-of-the-
Universe stride, he started for the executive elevator bay. As he arrived, the elevator doors
opened and Tess stepped out. She breezed right
past him.

"Tess," Benedict said.

She didn't stop.

"Tess?" Benedict said.

"You of all people should know, Terry," she
called back over her shoulder, "in your hotel,
there's always someone watching."

She kept going.

Benedict, now down a hundred sixty million

and one woman, boarded the elevator. Its doors closed on him with a silent swish.

The SWAT van doubled back toward the brightly lighted Strip, turned down an alley between gin joints, and ducked into a darkened warehouse.

In what seemed like no more than five seconds, the eight SWAT members reappeared, now all in suits, perfectly pressed. And with grins on their faces and change in their pockets, they emerged on the Strip and began their victory stroll, single file and sloppy.

Turk, Livingston, Frank, Basher, Yen, Saul, Linus, and Rusty marched down the Strip one after the other, looking at the sights, smiling.

And when they came to the famous intersection of Las Vegas Boulevard and Tropicana Avenue . . .

Virgil and Reuben, also in suits, fell into stride for a victory lap in front of the Bellagio fountains . . .

The MGM Grand lion . . .

The Mirage volcano, erupting in homage to them.

Then, one by one, the group splintered off, strolling into different hotels or grabbing cabs, until there were only two left: Rusty and Linus.

They took each other in, shook hands, and parted.

* * *

Tess barged through the Bellagio doors, emerging into the hot night. She looked around for Danny.

She dashed around the side of the building to a service entrance, where—yes! A Las Vegas PD squad car had just arrived to take Danny off the hands of the goons. She ran toward the police car.

"Wait!" Tess said.

They did.

But only to get Danny handcuffed and prepared for loading into the back of the squad car.

"Danny," Tess said, coming up to him out of breath. She held his glance. "I'm sorry," she said.

"I knew what I was doing," Danny said.

She looked at him.

"I didn't," she said.

A cop lowered Danny's head as he directed him into his seat.

"How long will you be?" Tess said.

"Three to six months, I should think," Danny said.

The squad car door closed him in and Tess stood vigil as it pulled away.

Across the street, Rusty, too, watched Danny being driven back to prison.

THIRTY-THREE

It was the same great metal gate that slid open to reveal Danny Ocean, ready for release a second time.

The same gray-green minimum-security prison.

The same view of New Jersey looking no brighter than it had before.

And again, no one was there to greet him as he took his first step into free America.

He got no farther than the first step when he discovered Rusty leaning against the prison wall. Beyond him sat his secondhand Mercedes from LA.

"Looking for someone?" Rusty said.

"Thirteen million," Danny said, "and you drive that piece of shit across country to pick me up?"

"Hello to you too," Rusty said.

They shook hands. Rusty looked Danny over.

"Your hair's grayer," Rusty said.

"Your eyes got closer together," Danny said.

A beat passed.

"How's life?" Danny said.

"Life . . . is a roomful of pillows," Rusty said.

A beat passed.

"C'mon," Rusty said.

They moved toward the Mercedes, together again.

"Where do you want to go first?" Rusty asked.

"To a phone," Danny said.

Rusty had anticipated this. "I stopped and picked up your personal effects, put them in the backseat," Rusty said.

"My what?" Danny said. He got to the passenger door and looked in to see Tess sitting in the back. She smiled at him.

Danny smiled back. "I'm not sure these belong to me," Danny said.

"Sure they do," Tess said.

Danny and Rusty got in.

Danny kissed Tess.

Rusty started the car.

"We need to find Rusty a girl," Danny said.

"There's a women's prison just down the road," Rusty said as he drove off.

In the back, Danny took Tess's hand in his. He noticed a silver wedding band on her ring finger. "You said you sold this," Danny said.

"That's what I said," Tess said.

"Liar," Danny said.

"Thief," Tess said.

As they drove away, another car started its engine and began to follow. Behind the windshield sat Benedict's goons, and as Rusty, Danny and Tess drove towards the Interstate, they remained a cautious distance behind them.